ON MY WAY HOME WHILE ANGER SLEEPS

Jason Ellis

ON MY WAY HOME WHILE ANGER SLEEPS

PAPERBACK EDITION

KINDLE ISBN 13: 978-1-906529-69-7

Dedications

For my family. I say that in every book, and I always will.
Tammy, Tyler, Mitchell, Bryce, and Kobi :)
We *really* are like the Weasleys ;)

••

This dedication differs from the Kindle version. You see, I
hatched a cunning plan recently ;) You remember that, don't
you, Jesse?
Now your name *is* printed in history, where I believe it should
be :) Keep inspiring, keep shining the guiding light, and just
keep being you.
Happy birthday x

••

Wait, there's another one? A secret one I haven't mentioned
before? Yes! ;)
Jes, from JesReadsBooks, shows us all so much courage,
humility, intelligence, and mental strength.
Recently, Jes has needed friends, real world and online, to
show how much we care and support her. I'm so glad, well,
honoured really, to call myself one of them.

Chapter one

A watched pot never boils. But … I need a cup of tea! A watched pot never boils. Of course it boils … it has to boil! If you're waiting for it to boil, because YOU REALLY NEED A CUP OF TEA, it will seem to take longer than usual. If I urgently needed a taxi, it would seem to take forever to pick me up as I watched out of the window. A waited for taxi never arrives. A watched pot never boils! I NEED A CUP OF TEA!

I stare at the kettle, tap my fingers impatiently on the kitchen worktop, and chant along in my head.

Finally, after four days of suffering from a vile sickness bug, I feel normal again. My temperature has lowered, the constant pounding inside my head ceased, and the cruel, violent cramps in my stomach have disappeared. I also feel confident that I'll be able to eat something more substantial than half a slice of dry toast, or a couple of biscuits. Plus, there'll be no more flat lemonade, or plain water. There will be glorious TEA.

BUBBLE … BUBBLE … BBUUUBBBBLLEE … CLICK!

I quickly pour the water into the eager cup, ready and waiting with a teabag and half a spoon of sugar in it. I add a little extra milk so that it is warm and immediately drinkable. I've waited long enough for this, thank you very much.

Oh-my-days … that is amazing. It's the best cup of tea in the world … the best I've ever tasted.

I finish my drink and make another straight away. I'll

1

take a little longer with this one, as I see how my poor stomach takes to scrambled eggs … on toast … with some butter! It has been beaten up by the bug, feels bruised, empty, and very unloved.

I sit down at the kitchen table, not mine by the way, my friend Amy's. We've been friends for so long, since we were younger children and lived only a few houses away from each other. I'm house-sitting for a couple of weeks while she is away on holiday with her fiancé's family. She gets to roam around Paris, and other parts of France, while I catch one of the worst stomach bugs I've ever had the misfortune to endure, and sleep in the hallway. I deliberately pulled a mattress out there, so I was near the bathroom. Disgusting and gross, I know, yet an absolute necessity over the last few days, trust me.

I'm in the middle of a break from work, so at least I don't have to worry about that side of my life as well. Exactly nineteen days ago, yes, I *have* been counting them, I left my job of three years as an administration clerk supervisor. It sounds much more important than it actually was. In two weeks time, I shall officially start my own business. I've saved wages, bought stock, set up my website and Etsy page, prepared a small room at home as my workshop and office, and posted everywhere I can think of across social media accounts.

'You're giving it a go, darling. You're forging your own path,' said my mum.

I might not sell a single piece of my handmade jewellery for weeks, months even, but at least I can say I'm the boss. It's all mine.

Scrambled eggs … on toast … with butter … and my ever faithful tea … I love you. At this moment, I really do, I'm not exaggerating.

The round analog clock, on the wall to my left, tells me it is twenty past ten. It is made of dark wood and copper, with large Roman numerals on the face, and is one of Amy's favourite items inside her flat. It's all cream and steel in the kitchen, so it stands out and gives the space a focal point. Even though she didn't plan it that way, and isn't strictly co-ordinated when it comes to interior design, each room in here carries the same effect. It's a kind of lucky style, unplanned and subtle.

The hallways throughout are all painted white, with stained skirting and door frames. They are very clean and precise, and welcoming in a modern way. I know there's an often used stash of emulsion and varnish, though, that other mere mortals aren't allowed to see. It is the truth behind the magic.

The lounge here is terracotta and light-wood, both bedrooms are maroon, cream, and white, and the bathroom a light-blue. The centrepiece in there? It's a rustic, hand carved, towel rack. Trust me, it works. I don't know how, but it works. At a past dinner party, I witnessed a twenty-five minute long conversation focused on that towel rack.

It is a beautiful home, and Amy is fortunate enough to own it. She is one of the managers at an accountancy firm. Great with numbers, equations, and money. Great with *her own* numbers, equations, and money.

"Well, I feel better, so I suppose I should rejoin the *world of the living*," I mutter to myself, in a slightly sarcastic tone, as I finish my tea.

I will admit freely, without any hesitation, that the recent sickness really did floor me. I haven't spoken to anyone since Friday. My days have been full of deep sleep, high temperature blurs, pain, and trying to find a positive angle, or attitude. I had reached a point when I was willing myself to be healthy once again.

I wash up my breakfast plate, then, with a slight grimace on my face, notice an odour in the air. *I hope that isn't me? Is it me? Uurrgh! It's ... horrible!*

I sniff under both my arms, and cup my hands over my mouth to check my breath. *Oh, it's gone. The drains, maybe?*

3

I'm only wearing a hip length, light-blue nightshirt, and that passes the test as well. It came out of my suitcase last night, newly washed and clean, carrying the scent of wild flowers and morning dew. Well, that's what the label on the bottle of fabric softener promised me.

Okay, Shayla, drink some more tea. Take a shower. Move the mattress out of the hallway. Oh, and don't forget to check your phone as well. It's been off for ages now.

Despite the wild flowers and morning dew, I want to start this day afresh. I feel much better, energetic, and charged. It is the wonderful sensation that follows any illness. It's just normality, *not* being ill, I know, but a few hours as an invincible superhuman won't do me any harm.

I take off my nightshirt and throw it in the washing machine. My lips immediately smile in a childish and mischievous manner because I'm completely naked. It's just one of my 'things', my cute and quirky traits, and it's been with me for about seven years, since just before I turned twenty.

I was dating, and sort of in love with, a twenty-four year old named Josh. He was an intellectual, jet-black haired, handsome, intense guy. His dark brown eyes caught me in seconds, pulled me in, made my heart beat faster.

Oh, Josh, you horny beast.

We met in a bookshop, both of us browsing because that's what we wanted to do. Neither of us had a specific title on our minds, we were just walking around the shelves slowly, enjoying being surrounded by the beauty of all the words, and drifting away with our Rory Gilmore spirit animal. I would later discover a Charles Dickens portrait tattoo on the top of his left arm.

Josh lived in town, about ten minutes away from my house. I'd never dated anyone who lived in their own place before, and even contemplated dropping hints about moving in with him, although they never left my own inner monologue. Unfortunately for us as a couple, thankfully for me as a shy and naïve young woman, already giving my heart away, Josh's libido couldn't stay anchored.

I got out, wounded, betrayed, covered with all the usual clichéd emotions.

Oh, Josh, you over-horny beast.

I *was* naïve. I knew that I was. It didn't stop me falling, though. We used to walk around his flat completely naked as well, hence my current smile. Once that front door closed, it was our little piece of the world. The thought of, *and opportunity for*, sex at any given moment was always there, always dancing inside our heads. After a couple of months, I lost count of the times the opportunities became the genuine act.

How did this exciting and passion fuelled relationship meet its tear stained end? Well, in Josh's eyes, I became … ordinary, an everyday part of his life. I lost the 'thrill' element. The unexpected thoughts and urges morphed to a routine, and Josh wasn't ready for that. I think routine, in any form, was a terrifying concept for him. He needed the next adventure, even though the current one was still playing out. I mean, he'd started and not completed two different degrees, tried to be an artist, a poet, and a musician. I suppose the signs were there for me, in dazzling high-definition CGI, if I'd wanted to pay attention.

Oh, Josh, you over-horny, cheating, beast.

Secretly, I thank Josh sometimes. You learn from your mistakes, as the saying goes. I've only had four relationships since, and I am now a … *cautious* dater. I'm single at the moment, I've chosen to be for a while. You're going to have to be something special to change that, as *another* saying goes.

I walk through to the spare bedroom, grab a red top, jeans, and some underwear from my suitcase. Before I dress, I take a quick look in the mirror, just to reassure myself that I don't look ill any longer.

You've lost weight and your skin looks sweaty. Your eyes look terrible. Your hair needs a serious wash, Shayla. Sort it out.

"Whatever," I snap at my negative remarks. I've always had a bit of an interesting relationship with mirrors, and how I see myself. I mean, who hasn't, right? Male or female, at some point in time the reflection will piss you off.

"Let's try this again," I declare. I use the most positive, defiant, and in control tone of voice I can find. For a millisecond, I'm sure the unexplained and rancid odour returns around me.

Okay, yes, your hair needs a wash, but it's fine. My eyes will lose the bloodshot lines and return to their glistening white and golden-brown in no time. If I have lost weight, then yay for me. The skin on my face, especially around my eyes, has lost the sickly ashen coating, regaining some of its tone, plus my tan from the late summer is still lingering about.

"Beautiful," I say with a smile. A smile I notice has a small piece of toast stuck between a couple of my teeth. "Oh, whatever."

••

"That's very strange."

I stare at the answering machine in the lounge. Not a single phone call in four days. All the digital readouts in front of me display zero. No calls, no messages.

When I knew I was ill, last Friday evening, I called my mum and sulked for ten minutes or so about being sick. I told her I was going to turn off my mobile, so I could properly rest without interruption, and instructed her to use the landline if she needed to reach me. If I'm ever away from our home, it's rare that we don't speak for more than two days in a row.

Turn your mobile on. She probably forgot what you said and left a message on it.

I grab my mobile phone from on top of the bedside cabinet in the spare room, now with its mattress returned to the bed frame, remade with clean sheets, pillowcases, and duvet cover.

As I sit back down on the beige sofa, my mobile phone buzzes and beeps in quick bursts. I see email notifications, app updates, calender reminders, and the missed calls I wanted. No messages, though. I thought Amy would have telephoned for a chat by now as well. She sat with me a few weeks ago and explained, in detail, how she had altered and checked, *and rechecked*, her overseas calls and messages costs. The word strange dances inside my mind once again.

I tap around on the screen, activate the speaker phone, and wait to hear Mum's voice.

"You have four new messages," states the male voice. It sounds slightly robotic.

"Shayla, darling, it's me," begins my mum. "Are you feeling better? Listen … erm … can you give me a quick call back? Please do. I've gone and lost Amy's number somewhere in the kitchen. I'm terrible with bits of paper, aren't I? I put them down and they just disappear forever. It's nothing to worry about, but there were a few fights around here last night. Terrible bloody ruckus there was. I'm fine … I think I've just given myself the jitters, that's all. Bye, darling."

Poor Mum. She's so scared of anything like that.
The call log tells me that she phoned on Saturday, mid-morning. I immediately feel sick again. It's not because of the bug, it's pure guilt and concern. I deliberately turned off my phone. I didn't think she would lose Amy's number, even though, as she just said, I know fully well that she puts pieces of paper down and they disappear forever.

It's okay. Think, Shayla, think! The next message will be her telling you not to worry, right? She would have popped next door to Joan's house, had a nice cup of tea, and calmed herself down. You'll see. Her nerves are fully restored to their normal state, not 'all jangled up'.

7

"Next new message."

"Shayla, darling, it's happening again! What is going on around here? Maybe it's just one of those weekends when everyone has a bit *too* much fun. I just wish they weren't making such a terrible noise. It's like … a … a growl. Is that what happens these days? People get drunk and growl through the streets?!"

I can't be one hundred percent certain, yet I'm sure I hear a noise in the background, picked up on my mum's phone. It sounds horrifying to me, like a furious roar, animalistic even, full of … hatred.

"Anyway," continues Mum, "you rest up and feel better. Joan has locked her place up, and she's coming round the back way so we can sit in the kitchen together, *and* ignore all of this nonsense. Bye, darling."

My body lifts an inch with relief as I hear Mum's more jovial tone. At least she wasn't alone and scared. Joan and my mum have had many enjoyable evenings together over a few pots of tea, laughing, and usually moaning as well.

That was Saturday evening, just after nine. I need to check the news, and my social feeds. If there was a lot of trouble, it would have made someone's timeline. Nothing like a bit of exciting drama to create some compulsive viewing, grab some ever needed likes, and probably start a massive point of view argument as well.

'Hun, there just having fun! Don't get on your high horse about it!'

'Hey, hun! I'll post what I want. They're being disrespectful and childish! You wouldn't understand, I was brought up in a different time.'

'What?? You're only three years older than me, hun! And don't start about how I bring up my kids!'

8

'I didn't mention your kids! WTF?!'
Block. Unfollow. You know how it goes.

The robotic male tells me that the third message was left on Sunday morning.
What? Four o'clock in the morning? Why would Mum be up at that time?
I decide to grab my boots, my coat, jump on the next train back to Southend, and go home to check on my mum. I'm only a couple of stops away here, in Rayleigh. I can be there in twenty minutes, as long as the trains play along.

"Are y ... you caught up in all of ... of th ... this?" whispers my mum's petrified voice.

What the hell? Mum? Caught up in what?
I hear the roar, louder this time. A door slams, then another. Mum breathes, as if the phone is held close to her face. Glass smashes, and she inhales a screamed gasp, as if she urgently needs to silence herself.

Mum! I'm on my way! Fuck! I'm on my way, right now! What the hell happened?

I sprint from the lounge to the kitchen and grab the small bunch of keys off the worktop, trying to keep my thoughts in check. I fail immediately.
Calm the fuck down, Shayla! Put the keys in your bag ... go and get your bag! Are your boots on? Put your boots on! That's all you need ... you have money in your bag ... your bag ... go and get your fucking bag!

"Next new message."
That voice is really starting to piss me off now!
I hear footsteps from my phone's speaker, yet no voices at all. They are slow and nonchalant, as if they aren't

9

heading anywhere in particular, simply moving on the spot. A gruesome roar and heavy breaths stop me in the lounge as my heart jumps inside my chest, and my legs lose all their strength. I literally drop back on the sofa as my knees buckle.

"End of messages. To return to the main menu, press the star key. To hear the messages again …"

"SHUT UP!"

I push on my mobile phone's screen as hard as I can, wanting it to shatter beneath my thumb. I sit in a sickening yet needed silence, lost in time, lost between racing heartbeats.

Go, Shayla! Take a deep breath, or take ten, and GO!

Chapter two

I can't stop the vile and cruel thoughts as they mercilessly
crash, swirl, claw, and punch their way through my
imaginative mind. There are just too many of them, and they
are overpowering me with a masterful ease. All are dark,
horrible, violent, and vivid, centred on my mum and those
vague messages. Yes, they *are unthinkable,* they shouldn't have
even been given the spark of life, yet crash, swirl, claw, and
punch they do, defying their own description. They're
creeping through me, clinging to my blood cells as they swim
through my rapid heart, invading every part of my body, and
wrestling away control of my actions and behaviour.

Amy's flat is on the ground floor of a converted
warehouse building. There are two entrance doors, plus an
exterior thick gate made of iron. It provides access for the
residents, an extra point of security, and leads to the gardens
and parking spaces at the back of the main property as well.

There's that hideous smell again. It's so much stronger out here!
I think as I bound towards the second door, the one that leads
outside from this hallway, a communal area of the building. I
almost knock over one of the potted plants on a small table in
the corner as I power along.

My phone is pressed forcefully against my ear as I try
to get hold of my mum. It just keeps ringing, though, taunting
and scaring me with no reply.

'Hi, it's Shayla and Megan Dawson. We're not here at

the moment. Leave a message, or try our mobile numbers. Speak soon!'

I'm not one of those people, those that feel awkward when they listen to the sound of their own voice played back on a recording. I do not like my own voice right now, though. I definitely don't want to hear it. I want Shayla on the other end of my phone to piss off, if I'm honest. Shayla on the other end of the phone is the last person I want to hear from.

I end the call and jump ahead of the situation in my mind. *Just get the police. Get them now!*

The thought of having to involve police officers in a search for my mum sends an uncontrollable jolt of nerves through me. My hand shakes, I stop to hold the wall for a second to steady myself, then I drop my phone in the hallway.

Shit! Keep calm, please ... you can do this! my head screams at me, blatantly lying. I can't do this. I'm a nervous wreck. I'm the shattered sculpture of my own body, pieced back together and held there with the cheapest glue the artist had nearby at the time. At any moment, even from the slightest of touches, I'll crumble to a useless mound of dust, then blow away on a gentle breeze.

Breathe.

I breathe.

Pick up your phone.

I pick up my phone.

Breathe again.

I breathe again.

Call the police.

I call the police.

No answer.

What? There's always an answer when you call the police, isn't there?

I try again, telling myself I'll get an immediate response this time. They'll send every officer available to my house and find my mum. Armed emergency units, or whatever they are called, twenty or so police dogs, a few riot vans, a couple of helicopters in the sky. Yeah, that's where my imagination is running off to.

No answer.

Shit!

The door slams shut behind me and I turn towards the gate. I must have tears in my eyes because the cold November air hits my face, stinging my skin with an instant brutality. The damp and icy weather doesn't care about me, my urgency, or my fears. It isn't going to rip a gap through the grey clouds above and pull the sun over me.

I hear a car alarm in the distance as I head towards the gate. My body wants to run so that I can get home, however, it suddenly won't allow me to move fast. It is acting like a strange sort of barometer, warning me about incoming storms. Something isn't right. There's an unseen sense of danger out here. It is invisible, floating through the air, wrapping itself around me with limbs, hands, and fingers of pure ice.

I stare through the gate's bars, my view somewhat hindered by the house wall to my left, and the other to my right that surrounds the parking bays.

What's happening out here?

There's an abandoned car in the middle of the road. Its windscreen has been smashed but there is still half of it in place, the headlights are on full, and the driver's door is hanging open.

I think of my mum's messages. She told me there had been a lot of fights near her at the weekend. *Perhaps it wasn't just by Mum? Was there some sort of ... mass riot? Some unplanned mayhem that spread through the towns?*

I remember watching scenes from the London riots on television, back in 2011. I couldn't believe how quickly the chaos escalated and spread through the city. I've seen the same in other countries as well, on the news and the internet. When the spark is lit inside people, once it begins to fuel the passionate fire, it is rapid and often impossible to contain.

The motive could be justified or unjustified, the cause followed by one person, or by millions. What matters is the hope it instills within, the emotions it awakens.

I let my fear take control of my body and its immediate actions. It's been begging for complete command since I left Amy's, wanting to decide when I walk and when I don't, wanting to steer me along a safe path.

I'm allowed to move quietly and very slowly towards the gate, only breathing in silent, steady bursts.

Oh, Mum ... please be okay ...

My eyes blur the bars that are inches in front of me. They scan the viewable part of the street beyond, trying desperately to register everything.

Wh ... what the ...?

My thoughts are speechless, well, thoughtless. I can't comprehend this devastating scene.

My eyes dart at light speed, left and right. I see more abandoned cars on the road, rubbish strewn everywhere from ripped bin bags, smashed windows on houses, front doors kicked open, even lamp posts pushed over so their inner wiring is visible. They are like veins and arteries draping loose after a gruesome injury. The tarmac paths at their bases are torn open like a fresh wound.

Shit ... I ... I don't understand ...

I can hear flies buzzing loudly close by, lots of them by the sound of it. My mind wanders off on a tangent for a brief second, towards the hibernation patterns of flies, however, if I suddenly had all this rubbish, mess, and rotting food to party in, I'd probably wake up.

I look up the road towards the train station, where I should already be. My fear won't allow me to even consider it, though. It's grown an unwanted second skin, one of self-preservation, one that inexcusably cares for me more than it does my own mother.

I can't move, Mum ... I'm so sorry ... I can't fucking move! Please, let me move!

I'm ruled by fear. I can only tell myself that I need to be selfish right now, to try and understand what is going on. If I don't manage to stay safe, in the long run, I won't be able to help Mum.

A tear falls down my face and dances over my quivering lip. *I'm a coward. I'm a cowardly, shitty, crap daughter.*

I fight back. I fight with every part of myself I'm still in possession of. It feels like I'm walking through thick tar, my arms chained together and weighed down.

As I reach the gate and grab the bars, preparing to unlock it and pull it open, more of the devastation comes into view. My eyes lower to the path on my left. I feel my pupils strain and dilate with shock, and I hold my breath in a strange manner, as if I'm trying to play with time. I want it to reverse, speed up, or freeze in a safe moment.

There's a dead body on the ground … a dead woman … she's … actually dead … in a pool of her own blood.

My eyes know exactly what they are fixated on. They shouldn't be seeing what they are, nor do they want to stare any longer, yet my body won't move. I try to run backwards, jump away to the side, even open the gate and throw myself forwards.

Nothing.

I am a useless, cowardly, shitty, lump of crap daughter flesh.

There's a dead body outside the gate. Her bloodshot eyes are looking at me …

"Subconjuctival haemorrhage," I say in an airy voice, quoting one of those strange facts that everyone has stored in their brain. They often come to light at the most inopportune moments.

When I've witnessed such irregular knowledge being spoken by others in the past, I've rolled my eyes at them, wondering why they chose to open their mouths and contribute. I guess it could be some sort of defence mechanism? The brain is so shocked, or wanting for inclusion in the conversation, or desperate to impress, that is raids the 'random' files for assistance.

Get back inside!

I turn and fall awkwardly, bending my left knee the wrong way. My right leg skids forwards and I end up with ripped jeans, blood on my knee, and I overstretch my hamstring as well.

For a few seconds, I stay there in a numb cocoon. I am surrounded by the now explained stench that bewildered me earlier this morning, and I can see hundreds of flies crawling over the dead woman's neck and face.

Please ... someone ... help me ...

My heart is beating so fast I feel light-headed, and I'm gasping desperately for air. My stomach turns over and I retch, loudly, as well as making other whimpering, petrified noises.

I pull myself up using the wall and limp back to the outer door of the building. My fingers fumble wildly in my jacket pocket for the keys.

"Come on!" I scream. "Come on! Find the keys!"

Chapter three

I ignore the differing pains in both my legs and rush back along the inner hallway, heading desperately for Amy's. The real world is behind her door, *the safe world,* not this broken and unrecognisable version. I understand why I am homing in on it.

> *Call the police!*
> "Call the police!"
> *Get help!*
> "Get help!"
> *Help!*
> "Help!"
> *HELP ME!*
> "HELP ME!"

Strangely, such is my confused and terrified state, I don't recognise my own voice as it screams out all the petrified words. I literally believe, for a second or two at least, that I am not alone. Someone else is here and calling through the building.

I repeatedly bang my hand on the front door of flat number one. "HELP!" I cry, then run further up the hall.

"Call the police! POLICE!" I yell as I pound on the door of flat two.

I start up the stairs, not waiting for any kind of response from Amy's neighbours. I stop for a moment and yelp as my knee shoots with pain.

"Are you there? Help! Call the police! Something's happened! Someone died! SHE DIED!" I scream at the doors of flats five and six.

I rush back down the stairs as I try to get Amy's keys ready in my hand.

Where are you all? Where the hell has everyone gone? I think as I get back to Amy's front door.

It dawns on me, as I fumble and scrape at the metal lock and paint on the door directly around it, that I can't recall what any of the neighbours actually look like. I've met them on plenty of occasions before when visiting here. We've talked in the hallways, the car park, and even socialized at a few parties. My mind has deleted that information, or moved it to a different part of my brain, possibly seeing it as useless right now. Shock can change people in so many ways, I guess it has chosen to carve at my memory. For all I know, the dead woman outside lives here.

Used to live here. She's dead now. Dead. SHE IS DEAD.

I hobble back across to flat three and hit the door with my palm. It swings open and touches on the inside wall, very gently. As it is set out exactly the same as Amy's, only in a mirrored sense, I can see all the way down the hallway to the kitchen. There is a sense of familiarity because of this, maybe even of safety as well, yet I can't bring myself to move any closer.

My loud cries and shrieks disappear from my throat completely. Less than a minute ago they were echoing through the building at an incredible volume.

"Are ... are you in there? Hello?" I whisper. It has become difficult to force words out.

I actually don't want to hear an answer at all, I fear one. How would I even be able to speak to another person?

The world, my immediate world, is in ruins. Something happened. Something really ... catastrophic ... happened. I need to know more, find some answers, and try to understand any reasons. Then, and only then, will I be able

18

to think straight, *and* get back on the path to rationality again.

I rush into Amy's and slam the door behind me. I hear the same roar, the same growl, the same sickening sound I heard on my phone when my mum left me those heartbreaking messages. It isn't close by, though, it's distant, somewhere outside and to the right of the building.

What the hell was that?!

I knot my fingers together and pace a few steps, unsure how my body wants to react. I'm losing a critical mental battle, and I know it as well. Instinct, fear, and disbelief are keeping me on my feet, yet I'm expecting to fall into a corner and cry uncontrollably. It feels close, as if it is a set point in my future. I can't stop it from happening, no matter what I do to try.

Drink! Get a drink! It will help your nerves!

I agree with my thoughts completely as I try to piece my jigsaw of a brain back together.

Okay ... I've been here hundreds of times before. So, why can't I remember where Amy keeps her alcohol? It's ... erm ... it's in ... SHIT!

A couple of years ago, just as I was about to fall asleep for the night, I received a panicked phone call from my friend, Emma. Her boyfriend at the time, now her fiancé, Taurai, was in a car accident. I was devastated on hearing the awful news, however, I knew I had to be there for my friend when she needed me. Emma was inconsolable on the telephone back then, spluttering out broken sentences and details. She was frantic with worry, nauseous, and trapped deep inside a panic attack that seemed to offer no escape. She *really* needed me.

I knocked back two generous glasses of vodka and orange, then jumped in a taxi to the hospital. As I stayed by her side through the entire night, I was the voice of reason, of calm, of support, and of positivity. Okay, I know a couple of vodkas didn't make me act that way, *being me* made me act that way. Still, my brain truly believes it will help, so it *will* help.

I know where the drink is. I remember!

I go to the lounge and grab a bottle of brandy from the cabinet next to the sofa. I won't neck it neat, despite a strong urge to pour every last drop down my throat, so I take it through to the kitchen and grab a bottle of Pepsi and a glass.

Brandy is my favourite, if I am ever drinking alcohol. The odour from the bottle alone snaps me to confront this moment, and the abhorrent panic it has spawned.

The glass of drink has a soothing quality as I swig it on my way back to the sofa. It's as if I have just drunk a dose of reality, in liquid form, and it is calming me from the inside. My head is pounding, as is my heart, yet my thoughts are noticeably slowing down, dampened by the hit of brandy on my recently mashed up, sickened and very empty, stomach. I even imagine them as little people, swimming in a pool as the wave machine is turned on. They are thrown about, becoming one of many bodies, all floating and splashing wildly as the current grabs hold.

Is this what happens to my mind now? Is this a sign? I start drifting towards a kind of daydreaming madness? Will I eventually be sent over the edge of a ... psychological cliff ... caused by everything I've seen this morning?

I ring my house again, desperate to hear my mum's voice. No answer. Tears line my lower eyelids. I close my eyes and hear the strange growl inside my mind.

Get up! Do ... something!

I move across the room to Amy's computer and turn it on. The television remote is on the desk, so I push the power button on that as well.

I start tapping my fingers on the computer desk, half in a rhythm, half through sporadic and anxious jolts.

Local news? Google? Police website?

Unsure of exactly where to start, I click open the browser and add a few extra tabs. I search Southend in the first, load Facebook on another, and type in police on a third.

The television screen is blue, and there's a message on it notifying me that there is currently no signal being received. I tap a few buttons, yet all I get is the same message, or variations of it.

There has to be something here. Please …

Nothing stands out from my basic search on the computer. I was hoping for a massive headline that would explain everything to me clearly. Yahoo, BBC, and Sky news are all online, although the headlines and thumbnails are still from the weekend. The most recent I can see are from Saturday afternoon.

The police website only shows a welcoming statement from the District Commander, so I'm relying on social media to enlighten me.

I log into my Facebook account, not that I'm especially active there, and grab my phone as well to open Instagram. I click the 'most recent' link on Facebook and wait as it quickly refreshes.

Saturday … Friday … Friday … that's it? It can't be! Nothing after Saturday morning? That isn't possible.

Instagram suddenly offers me a lifeline as I scroll to a couple of posts, one from a clothes shop in Southend High Street, and the other from the local university. I can't quite believe I am looking at such an array of different photographs. There are book covers, thumbnails from Youtube videos, and new furniture, occasionally separated by smashed windows, what seems to be a raging fire, and a badly cut hand. I read the text under the latter.

'Member of staff injured while trying to secure the building! We're hearing reports of other such attacks in the town. Stay safe! Please!'

This … this can't be … real …

I finish my drink and go straight through to the kitchen again to pour out another, this time with more brandy than Pepsi. It's helping, even if only to dampen my intense and fearful thoughts.

Shayla ... seriously ..., I think to myself with dread, ... *what are you going to do?*

I have no answer to my own question. I can't even imagine the next ten minutes in this surreal and violent nightmare that I find myself a part of.

What are you ... GOING TO DO?

I blurt out a cry and tears flow down my face. I hunch over, hold my stomach, and grab the worktop for support. The breakdown I feared and sensed so forcefully is threatening to strike. All I want to do is crawl into the fetal position and let my emotions win.

No, Shayla. NO!

I grab my phone and try the police again. Still no answer.

I hit the screen of my phone with frustration, then try Amy. Nothing.

I try Joan, our neighbour and my mum's close friend, and berate my own stupidity for not calling her earlier. Mum said in one of her messages that they were together, so they might be at her house.

Again, sadly, just the ring tone and no voices.

I remember the hallway, when I literally directed myself through every moment, step by careful step, after I'd dropped my mobile phone.

Windows, yes ... the windows. Check that all of them are shut ... and make sure you are as safe as possible inside.

I am suddenly offered a barrage of horror movie scenarios by my mind. Any film I've watched in the past, specifically those including a character being alone and terrified, usually a teenage girl, replays a clip. *Does Amy own a baseball bat?*

I can't see much from the kitchen window, just along the back gardens of the neighbouring houses. I notice that a few doors are open, and some of the fence panels are down as well.

Everything is so close to me! How did I miss this? I know I lost hours and hours because of the sickness, but surely I would have heard something?

I move to Amy's bedroom, realising that her curtains are pulled closed. I carefully move with slow steps, short breaths, and reassurances of courage. I know the woman's body, the dead body covered in flies, is out there. She's about thirty feet way from the window.

Oh …

It's a rubbish thought, it doesn't quite fit the situation in front of me at all. This scene is deserving of a much more grandiose statement, yet it is the only one I could manage.

I feel sick …

I am bombarded with a broken landscape, framed by the window, a multiplication of my earlier glimpse through the bars on the gate. More details present themselves with violent force, unwilling to give me any time to prepare myself.

I notice more cars all along the road. At some point over the last four days they have been abandoned and smashed up somehow. People even parked them so they were across the front doors of houses.

Acting as a kind of makeshift barrier, I guess? What were they all so … so afraid of?

I can't see, or hear, any other people. At this time of day, nearly noon, there would usually be a throng of lunchtime students from the local school, mums walking along with their babies in pushchairs, people carrying shopping bags back to their houses, and cars driving along the roads.

I feel helpless and alone and afraid and sick and vulnerable and miniscule and worthless … and … I can't breathe! I can't … breathe! SHAYLA … BREATHE!

I smack my hand on the windowsill, hard. It hurts and a shot of pain clasps around my fingers, *however*, I'm gasping for air. My legs regain some essence of their strength and solidity.

23

I stare at a silver BMW, about one hundred feet away on the opposite side of the road. It has been reversed right up to the front of a house, and it makes me think of the door here.

I rush around the flat, looking at every item of furniture I can, deciding whether or not it will fit my panicked needs.

I stop at the small refrigerator in the kitchen, but worry about all the food and drink I'd inevitably waste if I unplugged it. I imagine myself here tomorrow, the day after, maybe even in a week, still alone, still without any idea about what has happened.

Don't think like that! Don't!

I move to the lounge and grab at the bookcase. *Come on! Move!*

I push it, pull at it, dig my boots in the carpet and grit my teeth, however, it doesn't move. It's too weighed down with hundreds of hard covers and paperbacks. I empty the top shelf with one hand and arm, sweeping the books to the carpet in seconds. It lightens the load and I start dragging the bookcase down the hallway.

I'm thinking about where to position it, and the best way for me to carry out such a task without getting stuck, when the security lens in the front door sparkles and catches my eye. I move slowly forward as a recent, albeit blurred, memory about flat three returns.

I peer through. The door is still open, exactly as I left it.

Where the fuck did everyone go? Where?

I go back to the kitchen and scan across the worktops. I grab an orange, an apple, and a small bag of pasta. My eyes are drawn to Amy's cooking knives, set out in a wooden block next to the blender. I grab the meat cleaver, surprised by its weight, comforted by its rigid sense of power.

The corner of my lips twitch, hinting at a smile. I just flashed back to a few months ago when Amy was hacking at some steaks. It's strange, because the portion of my memory concerning whether I stayed with her that evening for dinner has been lost.

Am I losing my mind? What's happening to me? I can't seem to remember anything at the moment!

I do recall that both of us were laughing hysterically as she called out the name of an ex-boyfriend, and one of his failings, with every swing.

'Tony, you were selfish in bed!' *WHACK!*

'Bradley, you bought me shit birthday presents!' *SWIPE!*

'Karl, you came round here with a bunch of lilies. I suffer from hay fever! You jerk!' *SLICE!*

I tip-toe back to Amy's front door and place my trembling fingers on the handle. All my movements are methodical, overly cautious, and forced to be silent as I turn the lock.

First of all, I listen. I stand there, completely still, for over a minute. I can't hear anything, though. No voices, no movement, not even the slightest hint of another person breathing. I know how loud I can scream, I know how much noise I made when I banged on all the doors in the building and called for help.

Is this some sort of … state of emergency? Maybe everyone was evacuated? But … why, though, and to where? I think, letting irrational, although still possible, thoughts to run through my mind. I'm bewildered by the state of the world after four days of illness induced sleep.

I underarm throw the apple down the hallway of flat three, watching carefully as it rolls towards the kitchen. It settles to an anti-climactic stop.

Why can't I remember what any of the people in this building look like?

The unknown neighbour doesn't come to investigate, and I can't hear any movement either. If an unexpected piece of fruit had just appeared inside my home, I'd flinch, or curse loudly, or jump out of my skin and throw the nearest heavy object.

'What the fuck! Why is there an apple rolling down the hall?' *Or something like that ...*

I do the same with the orange, adding more force. It hits the back door and bounces back a few inches. Still, nothing. No reaction, no investigation.

I move forward by a couple of steps and launch the bag of pasta. It lands outside the open door of the lounge, making a loud noise when it does. A crinkled thump echoes slightly, then fades away to eerie silence.

I move back to Amy's front door, waiting for someone to run out and confront me.

What do I do if someone is inside?

I wait for at least five minutes while trying to figure out an answer. During that time, rather foolishly, I stare without pause at an orange, an apple, and a bag of pasta.

I look at the hallway carpet for another twenty seconds, trying to notice any shadows inching their way to the left or right.

I tense my hand around the handle of the cleaver and walk forward. One step, breathe. One step, listen, breathe. One step, listen, breathe, grab the handle of the cleaver even tighter.

Remember, it's almost the same as Amy's. It's almost the same. Left is right, right is left. Just take it slow. Take it slow. Check the lounge first. Just poke your head around the frame. Run back if you need to ...

I can't tighten my grip, it's physically impossible. I still do it, though, causing tight pain to my palm and knuckles. I'm near the bag of pasta. I hear nothing. I see no signs of movement. It's quite dark, with only a few hints of light, so I guess the curtains are pulled almost closed.

I put my back up against the wall and inch along, glaring through to the lounge with wide eyes as it slowly becomes visible to me.

I'm so scared right now ... so scared!

I see smashed glass on the maroon carpet. I see family photographs thrown from the mantlepiece of the faux chimney breast, one that I know doesn't even contain a working fire. I see a handprint, created with something dark, sticky and congealed, smeared on the wall and the screen of the television.

Is that ... that blood?

I gulp in my scream, silencing it, and move fast. Once again I'm ignoring any pains I may have in my body. They are irrelevant in regards to my immediate safety.

I shut the door to Amy's and push the bookcase up against it. I'm thankful it is of a height that still allows me to manoeuvre my body and use the security lens if I need to.

I'm not satisfied and grab some of the books from the lounge, the ones I threw on the floor, and carry them back to add more weight to my makeshift barricade.

Shit! That was blood! Shit!

I sink to my knees, push my body up against the spines of the many books next to me, and know, without a doubt, that I'm about to lose some of my life to panic.

Why was there blood? Why? What the hell happened!

I read a book a year or so ago, and the main character theorized about fear and imminent madness. He was being haunted and, the 'short version' anyway, is that a person can only endure prolonged terror before their mind breaks, or they accept the situation *and* keep their sanity. I guess this is when I will test my own mental limits.

Okay, come on, stop ... think! THINK! Why? All the reasons why ... erm ... Zombie apocalypse? World War? A frickin' alien invasion? No! NO! Erm ... you're still ill? You are in a coma ... yeah ... a coma brought on by the illness. You're not here at all. You are in a hospital with intravenous lines poking out of your arms!

I will cry now, move mere inches in an agitated state, let twisted thoughts enter my mind, and cry some more. I don't have the emotional energy, physical strength, or courage to fight it off any longer. I believe I have reached my limit, *and* significantly passed it. There is no choice left open for me but to surrender.

At first, I imagine myself standing on the edge of a stoney cliff, although I am inside a large cavern. No sunlight, yet I can see, unable to understand how. The soles of my feet adjust to the gentle undulations beneath them, then I dive gracefully towards a deep-blue pool of water. My daydream soon changes, though, turning more macabre and dark. I start to flail, an expression of pure fear grows across my face, and I plummet at an unimaginable speed.

No ... please ...

My body whips over as I fall faster. I stare down to see that the beautiful water is now dark-red, sticky, and congealed as well, like the handprint.

I close my eyes, open my mouth to scream, yet I am consumed by the sickly pool of blood before I can make a sound.

Chapter four

I sank inside the dark liquid, the pool of blood, for almost an hour. I couldn't move away from the bookcase, nor did I have any real desire to do so. I sat down on the carpet and stared up the hallway with glazed eyes. It was an unhealthy amount of time for me to be inactive, too long trapped inside a shattered mind. I can't tell you, not with any clarity or honesty, if I will be able to recover.

As I stand in the kitchen, another brandy and Pepsi in my hand, I argue with my own thoughts. I have to decide whether or not to face my fears and head home, or stay here and try to find out what happened. Amy's is still safe in my eyes. It still feels safe around me. Fortified, sturdy, and separated from the rest of the world.

I stare out of the glass pane in the top half of the back door, across the car park. I can't believe it's the first time I've checked this view of the outside world. Perhaps I was too scared? Perhaps I wasn't prepared to face it after seeing the dead body earlier this morning?

How could this much damage … this much … I stop my train of thought, unable to find a word, or create a new one, that will fit the scene appropriately.

My mum liked to talk, *a lot*, about cause and effect, action and consequence, decisions and their outcomes. She had so many different ways to convey exactly the same lesson, or 'life message', to me. We watched all the Star Wars films together. Yes, she is a fan, yet she also wanted to teach me the Jedi way. I understand how friendship and love will always conquer dark magic, thanks to Harry Potter, Hermione Granger, Ron Weasley, and so many of the other witches and wizards in that world. There are two copies of each book in the series at home. We were enthralled by them at the same time while we read them together, and watched all the films as well. If I ever thought something was unfair, if I believed a decision needed challenging, I found my inner Katniss Everdeen, or Tris Prior. If I needed to rant, If I felt the urge to vent over anything, Mum would tell me to get it off my chest and 'not let it boil up inside'. She would sit and listen as I turned my metaphorical baseball cap on backwards and blurted it all out, Luke Danes style.

There were so many more examples from my mum over the years. They were usually offered to me in a subtle manner, yet always guided me to make the right choice, or walk the good path.

I try to make the right decisions. I try to make the right decisions … because I always aim for what is right.

Those words, decided on as a joint effort, are mine and Mum's. They are hand-painted, quite artistically, on a piece of wood we found on the beach, and it's hanging on the wall in our kitchen. The ellipsis is made up of three red hearts.

No, don't think about home …

As I see smoke drifting blissfully from a house in the distance, more smashed windows, violence, hatred, and vandalism the likes of which I couldn't have imagined before this morning, I cannot find a valid cause, action, or decision, that would have led to this. What could possibly have angered and scared people enough?

I scan through my list again to see if anything fits, even though they are all from the realms of impossibility. I mean, an alien invasion? Crazed zombies trawling the streets? I still can't believe any of them, despite being alone and surrounded by mayhem and a crushing solitude.

I've been angry before, of course I have. Everyone gives in at some point in their lives, *everyone*.

When I failed my driving test, I was angry. When I failed it for the second time, I was angry again. If memory serves, I kicked some clothes across the room and cried.

When Josh cheated on me, I was really angry. I cried, screamed, said shit and fuck a lot, and ripped up lots of romantic poetry he had penned for me. I remember being sick for a few days as well. Yeah, his behaviour actually made me throw up, mostly when I thought of the signals I should have easily noticed before.

When Dad left, I was really, *really*, angry.

Oh, Dad ... you ... you idiot! We loved you! We loved you so much! What did she have that we didn't?

That was the worst. That was when my anger kept screaming inside my head, unyielding, even dangerous. I threw a bottle of perfume across my room, one that *he* had recently bought for me. That trivial fact burned inside my heart with a fury. He knew. My dad knew he was going to leave and tear his family to shreds, yet he also decides to buy me a bottle of perfume? I couldn't get my head around that twisted thought process.

'I've been having an affair. I've chosen to leave my wife, to abandon my daughter, to change their lives forever. Oh, look, perfume. I'll just forget everything else and buy it.'

It shattered on my bedroom wall and slowly dripped down, meeting the hundreds of pieces of glass on my carpet. The stains looked mystical, like the fine membrane of a fairy wing, and they glistened in the light. At least I had a citrus and musky aroma in the air while I tried to understand his decision, and calm myself down.

But this?

This?

31

Why?

I grab my phone. I notice the time is twenty past one as I open the contact list and start dialling everyone in there.

Someone has to answer! I can't be alone in this! Someone has to be out there!

••

I am not only a cautious when I date, I am also cautious when I meet new friends. Due to this, running through my phone, from Amy to Zoe, takes me twenty-seven unanswered phone calls, and about forty or so minutes.

It's not long after two o'clock, Shayla. It's going to start getting dark in a couple of hours. You can't make it back to Southend while it's still light, the trains won't be running while all this is happening. I can't be walking around out there at night, I can't be.

I imagine Mum. I picture her in the same position, staring out of the windows, wondering how the world was ruined, begging that I'm okay.

But … she would have called by now …

"SHUT UP!" I yell at myself. I immediately grow angry and launch my glass across the room. It shatters on the wall, dripping Pepsi and brandy down in racing streaks. I think of my dad again, keeping the emotions boiling inside me. The glistening fairy wing looks darker this time, more sinister.

I'm sorry, Amy, I think to myself. I seem to be in the middle of an unexpected war-zone, yet I still feel guilty about making a mess in my friend's home.

I grab a tea towel and rush over to wipe up the ruined drink. I even think about getting the large pot of white paint out of the cupboard.

Unexpected and random thoughts appear in my head as the suspense movie clips return. This time, instead of the scared teenage girl wielding a baseball bat, she's becoming a master handywoman, cutting up wood, nailing it over doors and windows. In the space of a thirty second montage, wherever the stranded teenager is, it's turned into an impenetrable fortress, capable of withstanding any attempts to enter.

I think for a few seconds.

Those seconds turn to minutes.

I turn around and stare at the bookcase by the front door, fighting with all my mental strength to keep the pool of congealed blood, and another breakdown, at bay. I also move my eyes to the knife rack that provided me with my powerful meat cleaver earlier. An idea, a notion of safety, crosses my mind.

I drag the dining table in front of the back door, then pull the blinds down fully. I want something to cover the top part of the door, though, by the glass.

Is this what everyone else had to do? Did they grab furniture as well, petrified by the unknown threat?

I snap myself back from the unnerving daydream. I stack the microwave on top of the table, then put the blender on top of it.

I'm so sorry, Amy, again. So sorry. If this ever gets sorted out, I promise I'll tidy everything up …

Another memory about my dad surfaces, and I can't resist it. The whole situation crushed Mum and me, and I'm confident and accepting enough now to freely admit that. For close to a couple of months, though, we were empty vessels. The sudden change, the emptiness his departure created, it was impossible to accept.

I came home from work one day to find my mum upstairs, sitting on the landing. She was surrounded by sheets, the duvet, and pillows from her bedroom. She was crying and laughing as she wrestled with which emotion to listen to.

"We need to move my room!" she begged through tears. "I need … I need to change … I mean *a change*. You understand?"

I did. I fully understood the motivation and reasons

behind Mum's erratic and desperate behaviour.

We spent the next few days rearranging the house, moving furniture, and even redecorating some parts of it. Without speaking of Dad, unless by necessity or accident, we both moved items he had left behind, or those we owned attached to sentiment.

I was tempted to let my darker feelings win, on more than one occasion. I was tempted to throw everything of his out with screams of fury and disappointment, yet Mum carefully packed everything, or hid it away in cupboards. She used the time as therapy, as her chance to accept, start to heal, and begin to move on.

I try not to keep secrets from my mum. Yes, I have done it in the past, we all have, right? I try not to if it is avoidable, though. Lies are often painful. Lies are often dangerous. I mean, it is such a short word, only three letters. Lie. So powerful, though. Three letters that can cause damage beyond comprehension.

I'm sorry, Mum. I … I don't know … I suppose I didn't think you would understand … I didn't want you to get even more annoyed, or upset.

One of the secrets I have kept from her concerns the items we stacked away during that time of bitterness. My mum's old room became a place of clutter and storage, of dusty boxes, hidden feelings, and turned around photo frames.

I noticed you, Mum. I noticed how you glanced at the door, but you wouldn't ever go in. I saw your shoulders sink as you fought away the sadness.

I've taken objects out of that room, ones that either belonged to my dad, or that he bought for me or Mum. She doesn't know. In my mind, I thought it would … ease her pain, somehow. The less of 'him' the room contained, the less power it held, the weaker its influence would be. It couldn't hurt her as much.

I threw them away, or broke them first and then

threw them away. When I did, when I carried out and created my secrets, I would argue with the reasons for the gifts. Sometimes it would be a thought, sometimes a whisper.

'Dad, this watch was for my seventeenth birthday. It means nothing to me now. You have no right to any of my birthdays any longer.'

I threw that watch in the sea ...

'You were a superhero to me, Dad. You were a *real fucking superhero!* Now, I ... can't stand to think of you. I bought you this Superman cup for Father's day, three years ago. You don't deserve it, I take it back.'

I smashed that with a hammer from your toolbox.

I can't help but wonder where he is right now. The depth of my feelings try to force some emotions, yet I remain indifferent. Proof, I suppose, of how much he hurt me? Of how dangerous those three letters really are?

As I reach the kitchen window, I check the back gardens in view. There are a couple of security lights on, although I can't remember if they were like that earlier.

Shayla, don't you want to see outside? Don't you want to know what is happening?

I want to ignore that thought. I *really* want to ignore that thought. The answer is both yes and no. The memory of the dead woman's eyes and her subconjunctival haemorrhage don't want me to look out of another window for the rest of my life, or leave this building ever again.

I step backwards and pull myself up so I'm sitting on the worktop. I kick off my boots and stand up, barefoot. I'm five-foot-four, so there's a bit of room before my head hits the ceiling. I can see further along the back gardens, though, which could bring forth vital information. I don't want it to be true, yet this mayhem, this incredible display of brutality, it may not be over.

A distant growl sounds. *Again! That was somewhere outside the front of the building ... closer this time ...*

A tear falls from my eye. *Mum ... I ... can't leave ... I'm sorry … please be okay … please!*

I climb down from the worktop, wipe my eyes, and walk to the bathroom with guilt ripping at my heart. I can't let the thoughts in, I can't permit them to exist, even though they are becoming more truthful with every second that passes.

I hang a towel against the curtain rail of the small window in the bathroom, then head to the spare room.

Just cover the window … hang the duvet up there.

I look at the bed, however, I can't imagine myself sleeping, not even for a single second. *I'll move the mattress again. Maybe to the lounge? Or just rest on the sofa?*

I choose the sofa option, then head to the lounge. I seem to have decided, without remembering the action, that the curtains at the front of the flat will be left open, as well as the small window I'm not covering in the kitchen. They will provide me with suitable vantage points, and still keep me hidden, out of view in the dark.

If I sit up on the back of the sofa, I can see out and over the road. It's comfortable, unlike standing on the worktop, plus the headlights from the abandoned car are beaming directly around there. I doubt any of the toppled streetlights will come on later tonight. They are dead, destroyed, they are lifeless. *Yeah, just like the woman outside. She's dead. Dead.*

I enter Amy's bedroom, avoid getting too close to the window because of a possible sight of the dead body, and rearrange the pillows and duvet. I need a raised position.

Think, Shayla … is that everything? Is that all you can do?

I nod my head at my own answer. Then, I shake my head, rush back to the kitchen, grab the knife block, and begin to distribute the weapons throughout the different rooms.

Chapter five

It's nearly four o'clock, I am hiding in the lounge, and I haven't moved much in the last couple of hours. I'm examining the scene outside, begging for it to change. If I suddenly blink and wake up on the mattress in the hallway, I'll take it. I'll remember this as the most vivid dream in my lifetime and take it.

Please ... all just a terrible dream. I'll take it ... I'll even take the coma. I'll wake up six months in the fucking future, surrounded by tearful family and friends. Please. I don't care! Nurses and doctors can rush about as I open my eyes for the first time in months ... PLEASE!

I switched brandy out for tea after I placed knives in all the rooms, ate half an apple, and then an orange as well. I didn't actually feel hungry at the time, I still don't, but my head and stomach now both love me in equal measure.

The sun has almost set outside and there seems to be a link, or a reaction to it. The growls are louder and have become much more frequent, as if whatever made those noises sensed it. They actually sensed the change in daylight. What is strange, and terrifying at the same time, is that they remind me of documentaries I've watched in the past about pack animals. I hear a growl, I hear another, then another. They seem to be calling to each other.

I think werewolves hunt in packs, don't they? Vampires stalk their pray at night. Oh, whatever! As much as I am open to the supernatural, a pack of snarling werewolves didn't rampage through the streets over the past four days and trash everything. No. No. NO!

My list of impossible reasons grows and I shake my head in response, and annoyance, however, there has to be one. This strange event in the world deserves something equal to explain it.

I step down from the back of the sofa, grip my cleaver, and creep through to the kitchen. I snap a look at the carving knife on the table, letting it give me that millisecond of courage and safety.

The various aches in my body struck at me while I moved, so I have no choice but to stop and check on my injuries. Both my legs sting and throb, and the cut on my knee needs cleaning and a large plaster. My palms hurt as well, from when I banged on all the doors for help.

"Sort yourself out. You need to," I say as I rub my pulled hamstring. It isn't hindering my ability to walk, nor is my knee, yet they are both producing sharp and random pains.

As I clean the dried blood off my knee with a damp tea-towel, I wince. It's also reminding me of the handprint across the hallway, so I rush to finish up with some antiseptic cream and a plaster.

I climb up on the worktop, steady myself in my lookout position, and watch across the gardens and fence panels.

Nothing. The security lights are helping, but they're no good if there's nothing to even see. What is out there? What ... what are you?

Suddenly, I hear a new noise. It sounds like a digital alarm clock, or watch, beeping.

Is that in here? No, I'd have noticed it before today. One of the other flats in the building, maybe?

I carefully climb off the worktop, then walk through the flat with a new thought in my mind. I need to check everything electrical, just to make sure the same doesn't happen here. I'm still barefoot, so my steps are quiet on the carpet.

Once I'm satisfied that a random alarm isn't going to go off here, I stare through the security lens on Amy's front door. I'm relieved to see that the lights in the communal hallway are on. The door to flat three is still open, and I can just about see the bag of pasta I threw along the hallway earlier. It's still on the floor, by the lounge, seemingly untouched.

"Is it coming from in there?" I whisper. The alarm is definitely louder by Amy's door, and at an altered pitch.

For a moment, I daydream about my friend, Charlie. She has a physics degree and loves everything related to science. I'm sure her keen mind would have a few theories about all this, wherever she is.

Charlie is great to be around, and often explains everyday situations, or occurrences, with knowledge and reasoning. Thanks to her, I know this is an example of the Doppler Effect. Thanks to Charlie, I know the alarm is closer to me here than it was in the kitchen. I allow myself to step forward, up against the door, and move my eye closer to the lens.

Is that ... footsteps? Is someone else here? I think, feeling scared and relieved at the same time.

Then, the relief disappears. It is stolen from me in an instant.

The loudest roar I have heard since all this began punches its way along the hallway. I can even feel the sound on my palms, *through* Amy's front door.

NO!

I freeze on the spot and my heart feels as if it literally skips a beat. I seriously consider it to be a heart attack, just for a split second. It jumped, paused, then jumped again with a force that took my breath away.

My right hand plants itself on my chest, the other over my mouth to try and keep any sudden screams hidden as well. If the basic beep from an alarm clock caused this, what would a loud scream do?

39

I step back, unable to breathe. I force myself to inhale and step forward again straight away. I need to see this, to confront the fears, and try to understand the devastation I woke up to.

A short period of time follows, how long exactly I cannot tell you. It falls quiet except for the alarm clock, still sending its piercing tone through the air.

What's going on? What the hell is happening?

Then, I hear glass smash somewhere close by, plus loud bangs and crashes from across the hallway.

There's another roar, plus a sort of rasping and heavy breath, like a panting animal.

I see nothing. The hallway of flat three is dark and filled with shadows, although none of them are moving. I hear another thump, then the alarm stops.

Growl.

Rasping breath.

Distant footsteps on the street outside. They walk at first, then run.

An impossible silence follows. Nothing exists. My own heartbeat can't even break through. I have no words. I have no thoughts. I can't even imagine an explanation. My list of possibilities rips itself up into hundreds of pieces, and they all float away like small paper butterflies.

Check the windows! Grab the fucking cleaver and check the windows!

••

After all my preparations, both mental and physical combined, and the suspense movie recalls that supplied me with girl-stuck-in-a-house-alone-and-scared memories, I still betrayed all the characters in the genre. I'm a mess. I'm a nervous wreck. I am the shattered sculpture again, however, I've already turned to dust this time. I'm blowing away on the breeze.

It's now seven o'clock in the evening. I don't want any of the lights on, so it's dark here inside and out, and I am surrounded by shadows most of the time. They comfort and chill me equally.

If I had the ability to look at myself and my behaviour, from outside of my body, detached and ethereal, I'm unsure how I'd react. We have all screamed at a television screen in the past, be it at a show or a movie. We have all decided whether or not we will ally ourselves to a character, fight along with them as the plot unfolds, and sympathize towards their emotions. Of course, there's also a flip-side.

'Oh my days! Don't go down there, you stupid bitch! The killer's right there! He's got a knife!'

'Run! Hide! Why aren't you moving? Why are you just standing there?'

'What? Go outside to investigate the noise that sounded like someone snapping a neck? Erm … that's such a great idea!'

Yeah, to be honest, I think I'd be on the flip-side right about now.

Since hearing the unexplained rampage inside of flat three, I managed to crawl through Amy's to check the other rooms. When I say I managed to crawl, I truly mean it as well. I've moved slowly, my whole body shaking uncontrollably all the time, holding in fear induced stomach retches so I haven't made any sound. If something as mundane as an alarm clock caused the unseen horror to focus its attention here, then I will never let another word out of my throat.

What was it, though? What do I call this … thing? It has no name, no face … it is just an unseen … anger.

I made it all the way around the flat and eventually back to the lounge. Distant growls, roars, and … I don't know how to explain them … almost primal cries of rage, bombarded me constantly from outside. Some were close, some distant. There was something else in the sounds as well, though, like an emotion, or a passion. I've never heard anything like it before, which is why I can't process it properly.

The congealed pool of blood, thick and suffocating, is urging me to return. I've managed to resist it so far, although I do not know if I can last the entire night. Hearing those sounds, my body flinching, and my hand grasping the cleaver as every minute passes by, it's all too much. It is a nightmare. The word is often overused in modern times, banded around along with trivial situations.

'I've lost my keys, what a nightmare.'

'I'll be there in ten minutes, the traffic out here is a nightmare.'

'What a nightmare, Netflix is down and there's a new episode of Shadowhunters out!'

This is a true nightmare, one that has me fearing for the fragility of my life, my own mind, and I can't wake up from it.

Shayla … don't give in. Don't fall towards the dark pool again … don't … please …

Chapter six

I'm by the back door in the kitchen, crouched down on the floor by the table. I walked here, although I am unsure how. My legs have no feeling in them at all, no power, no will to be a part of the rest of my body. That's how I feel at the moment. I am separated, fragmented, and shattered. My mind remains in the lounge while my shell of a body moves to another room. Minutes later, I catch up with my confused thoughts and wonder when it happened.

I am thirsty, hungry, and beyond exhausted. There are gaps in my memory, times when it feels as if five minutes have passed since I looked at a clock, yet it has actually been forty. I may have closed my eyes, although it doesn't feel as if I have slept. I just can't be sure of my own actions, they aren't mine right now.

Drink, Shayla! NOW!

I take a deep breath, then another. I'm listening to myself, I hear my sincere and direct thoughts. Slowly, I obey.

I'm scared that the tap will be too loud if I get a glass of water. Will the fridge door bring ... *them* ... *the anger* to me?

Just be careful, Shayla ... and silent.

I choose the tap and pour out a large glass of water, expecting the front door to be torn off of its hinges. Fear is winning ... no ... fear *has already won*.

A screeching roar, coming from somewhere beyond the car park, forces my hands to grab my glass even tighter. I fear it will smash and cut me, but I can't stop. I falter backwards, my spine hits the worktop, and I stare out of the kitchen window.

You can do this, Shayla … you can. Climb up and have a look outside.

I allow myself a few moments to reassemble. I rub my arms and legs, trying to feel my own touch. It sounds strange, but I need to know that I am actually here. I begin to imagine cracks in my skin, healing and pulling themselves back together.

You are in the kitchen. You have a drink in your hand. You are in the kitchen. THE KITCHEN!

My body has never experienced prolonged fear before. It has no choice but to react in this manner, no comparison or knowledge of how to escape. I wonder if I have already passed my limit by a few mental miles. I haven't accepted any of this, so, according to the haunted main character in that book, my sanity is lost.

The clock on the wall surprises me. It is nearly three in the morning. *What? That … can't be?*

Reality slaps me across the face, pulls my eyes open, then reaches deep inside my chest to pump my heart.

I've been here nearly all night long? I've listened to the surrounding rage for hours? I think, stuck between contrasting emotions. I'm sickened by what I have experienced, yet empowered that I have also survived.

I climb up on the worktop and my ravenous eyes target the loaf of bread on the side. I grab a few slices and start to eat as I stand up. I have to hold the cupboard door for stability and even feel a little bit light-headed.

The security lights are glimmering over a few of the back gardens, streaking lines along the tops of the fence panels. There is a strange beauty out there, natural mixed with manmade. The leaves on the trees, bushes, and flowers in view sway gently, sparkling as if made of silver.

What the fuck is that? A shadow appears from inside the

patio doors of a nearby house. It's down the street, so I can't see much at all, yet it appeared normal.

Normal person, normal house, normal night. No, I can't believe that! Nothing about this world is normal any longer!

A dog barks.

The shadow flies down the garden.

The dog barks louder and is also snarling, as if preparing to attack. I think I hear wood snapping and splintering.

Complete silence.

I see a fence panel fall over.

I sit down, unable to piece whatever I just witnessed together. I'm trying to create the backstory, the plot, the reason why. Nothing fits. Nothing can provide me with the crucial details to tie it all together. However, the connection between sound and violence presented itself once again. It's almost a trigger, a lure.

I refill my glass, confident that the tap is quiet enough, and move back to the lounge. I seem to have found some energy, some renewed thirst for understanding. It is carrying my physical form along with it, so I don't resist.

The abandoned car has illuminated a large part of the road since sunset, not that anything has happened, though, not that I have seen. Whatever is roaming around outside on the streets, it is concealed, cautious, dare I even say it, intelligent as well?

You could … could test out your theory, right? Do they actually react to sounds?

"No," I whisper, scared by my own idea.

I sit up on the back of the sofa, eat more bread, and sip plenty of water. Once again, my body disappears through daydreams, broken time, and the orchestra of fury outside.

Chapter seven

Birdsong. I can hear it, can't I? It is real?

As I sit on the floor by the kitchen table, in an almost fetal position, I think I'm daydreaming about the peaceful and beautiful sounds. I'm unsure if the change in light through the room is a sleep deprived hallucination, or if sunrise has finally arrived.

The roars have stopped ... they're leaving, finally. I can only hear a few of them in the distance ...

I now fear the sunset. It is a new fear, raw, and still growing. I have no idea what is out there, but it created a guttural thunder that crashed throughout the night, an incessant chorus outside, and it chilled me to the edge of sanity and reason. Seeing the hints of daylight creeping into Amy's calms me, gives me an internal energy, a vigour, and slays some of my dread.

I pull myself up, hold the table for crucial support, then slowly remove the blender and microwave. They feel a lot heavier than they did yesterday afternoon.

You need to eat more ... and drink. Shayla, you need to get a hold of yourself ... please ... for Mum ... and for yourself ...

Thoughts of Mum cause the tears to flow freely. I'm not interested in stopping them, they deserve to be here on my numb skin, to be running down my face. Despite the terrors I endured during the night, I'm still a cowardly, shitty, crap daughter.

I grab my phone and ring Mum. No answer. I can't say how much of me knew there wouldn't be one, how much I believed it would be that way, yet it is becoming more accepted. It is another reason why I cry.

I open the fridge and take out a new bottle of Pepsi, not caring at all that it's only seven forty-five in the morning. I also grab some ham, bread, a block of cheese, and some peanut butter.

I enter an unusual, and also very unexpected, state of autonomous action. My body is suddenly on autopilot as I move around the kitchen, grabbing glasses and cutlery. My actions are kind of a blur, unregistered in my immediate and short-term memory, yet I know I'm making myself food.

My friend, Dean, I've known him since college, used to talk about 'autopilot' every time we went out to a club. He believed it helped him arrive safely home, regardless of the amount of alcohol he had drunk by the end of the night. It never failed him. I expect there's a scientific name for it. Some sort of 'homing' sense possessed by human beings.

I'll check that with Charlie. She'll know, or start researching the answer.

My lips sink slightly. *I won't be able to, though. Everyone has … they've gone … disappeared …*

I wipe more tears off of my face, swig some drink, and take a large bite out of a ham and cheese sandwich. My eyes peer through the blinds on the back door.

The car park looks exactly the same, doesn't it?

I try to remember, with as much detail as I possibly can, what it was like out there yesterday. It reminds me of a game I played at birthday parties, when I was much younger. You know the one I'm on about, don't you? I knew it as the *tray game*, or *what's missing?* Every kid memorises the objects, usually toys or sweets, on a tray. The mum, the dad, or the entertainer for the party, would then cover them and remove one. The kid who shouted out what was missing first won a prize.

Okay, I need to think. That blue car has moved, hasn't it? There's more rubbish on the ground ... wait ... the red bike has gone ... there was definitely a red bike!

I won't get a bag of sweets, or a small toy, but at least I know my memory isn't shredded, my mind isn't completely lost to me, not yet.

My eyes focus on the gate that leads out to the car park, swinging back and forth on silent hinges. It's beckoning me towards it, like a wooden hand waving me to join in with the adventure, to trust that it will be safe.

Mum, wherever you are, whatever happened, I'm on my way! I'm coming home. I'm a brave, not shitty, brilliant daughter!

I realise it's time to leave. No more fear. No more cowardice. I can avoid the dead body outside, make my way through the devastation in the streets, and get home.

I'm about to move.

That ...

I'm about to run out of Amy's.

... sounds different ...

I'm about to head home.

... like a ...

I'm about to find my mum.

... Oh ... no ... please ... no ...

I spent all night covered by a deranged coating of fear. The noise *they* made kept me trapped in a permanent and sadistically cruel panic. It was *nothing* compared to the fear I now feel. This fear cuts through me, grabs at my skin, and forces my heart to pump without mercy.

A different sound. A different cry.

My heart retaliates and pauses once again, desperate for its normal rhythm, and my imagination runs millions of images through my weakened mind. I'm suddenly writing possible futures ... my future, my story ... thousands of times. They all begin the same way, with the same opening words.

She heard a different cry ...

I hold my breath. Unlike in the alleyway yesterday, time does pause for me now. I exist outside of the normal universe, trapped between one second and the next, as the new sound haunts me. Yes, that is the best way to express the feeling. The only way. I am haunted.

My thoughts regain some of their control and swim along in slow motion, moving around and piecing the words together. They need to form something understandable from the fragments.

That sounds different, like a …

"Oh, no. Please, no," I whisper. "That's a baby. That's a crying baby."

Chapter eight

I don't believe my body has ever moved in such a precise manner before. I have the grace of a professional dancer, the speed of an olympic one hundred metre runner, perfect eyesight and coordination, plus a resonating calmness. It is holding me together, binding me as a complete person, a complete soul.

I was on the athletics team in year ten and am no stranger to training, or the capabilities of the human body. I was even chosen to represent them in nearly all school and borough sport events. This, though, is something new, something my body has never experienced before. The crying child is my only audience here, cheering me on to win with its desperate call.

I have to find the baby! I have to!

I navigate through Amy's home and perform a multitude of tasks on the way. I glide through doorways, jump over furniture to save time, and make sure to listen as well. I am always listening.

There is no hesitation this time, no doubt, no second thoughts. I am leaving, and I am going to find that baby. I am going to protect that baby from this new and devastated world. I know this is my safe house, my base, yet I must now venture outside.

Mum ... Mum! What do I do? I can't handle this! How do I ... I ... care for a baby? How do I ... become you?

I grab a pack of biscuits, a couple of chocolate bars, a few pieces of fruit, and some bottles of water. *That's enough! Just go!*

I already have a rucksack that I brought with me when I came to look after Amy's. It is still packed with a small selection of books, my Kindle, and some charging leads.

Shayla, darling …

I can hear my mum. Her voice is inside my head, answering my questions.

'I try to make the right decisions. I try to make the right decisions … because I always aim for what is right.'

I can see the homemade plaque in my kitchen, on a hook in the bottom of the wooden spice rack. There's a little jar of ground chilli powder on the bottom row, opened once, never touched again. We both thought it was too hot for our tastes.

I can see and hear my mum at the kitchen table, speaking those words out loud. She points to the plaque, doesn't make eye contact, and recites the advice perfectly. Her other hand is usually on the handle of her tea cup, or the teapot, placed on a crocheted mat in the middle of the dining table.

Thanks, Mum. I love you.

I drag the table across the floor, assure myself that I have everything I need, especially the meat cleaver I wrapped in a tea-towel, and open the back door.

The stench I was confronted with yesterday hits me again as I step outside, although it is not as potent. Fresh air has slightly diluted the odour, as if Mother Nature herself is fighting back against whatever monstrosity she is now faced with.

My senses are overloaded as I stand a few feet outside the building. I am unsure when, or if, I'll ever return here, so I focus for one more second and lock the door. All I truly want to do is examine every single piece of rubbish, every shattered shard of glass, every splintered panel of wood.

I want to pick them up, feel them in my hands, read their story, and possibly understand the anger that created them.

Up there … towards the train station! The baby is up there somewhere!

I throw the rucksack over my shoulder and start to jog across the car park. I plan possible routes as I dodge random debris and move between the smashed up cars. I can't quite believe that an entire hydrangea bush has been ripped out of a garden somewhere. It's deep-green and browning leaves, plus the remnants of blue petals, look strange and fantastical against the grey concrete. It is as if the entire scene has been painted on the ground to purposely stand out and catch my attention.

Before I can think about whether or not I will successfully jump over the fence a couple of feet ahead of me, my boot plants on it and I throw my hands up. They grab the top, grip tight, and pull me up.

Do it! Don't stop moving!

My legs spring to aid me with a boost. I do not understand this sudden flood of energy, yet I'm not going to question it either.

I'm coming … don't worry, little baby, I'm almost there …

I land in a neighbouring back garden and power across the lawn, forcing the world to blur all around me. I can't allow for distraction, I can't allow for anything to stop me from reaching the baby.

"Oh … fuck!" I shout as I trip over something and fall forward. My left wrist makes a terrible noise, as if I've just ripped a piece of meat apart with my bare hands. I drag in a few sharp breaths as the pain heightens.

"Shit! My wrist! I've broken my wrist!" I curse through gritted teeth.

Have I? Is it broken? Shit!

I lift up my forearm and move my hand around. It is swollen, painful, and it stings a lot, but it is still functioning as a normal wrist should.

I turn my head around. All the pain is pushed away by an army of disgust and fear. I start clawing myself across the garden, digging my nails into the hard and cold mud, clasping at clumps of grass, working only on instinct. There's a dead dog on the grass, a German Shepherd.

Oh fuck! FUCK! Get away! Get AWAY!

The dog is covered in blood, its tongue is lopped out of its mouth, and it has a large chunk of its skin missing by the neck. The brown and black hair is tainted with patches of dried blood, its lustre stolen.

I scramble to my feet and rush away. I'm moving backwards, unable to take my eyes off the dog's massacred body. The smell is horrendous and I have only just noticed that I am surrounded by it. My stomach flips and I retch loudly.

I turn and jump for the top of the next fence, however, the eviscerated dog has thrown me out of my forceful tempo. The sight of it has grounded me in a harsh reality, and its brutal hands are wrapped around my ankles, pulling me to the ground.

"Come on!" I scream.

I leap again and reach for the top of the fence panel. My muscles steady themselves, my lungs grab some air, then I pull my body up with all my strength.

The baby cries as my boots hit the grass. I've almost made it, almost succeeded in my role as a protector, as a guardian, as a …

No, don't think it, Shayla …

"Mum," I whisper.

The garden here has been damaged, although not as bad as the outside streets. The bench and outdoor dining set are both bent up, their metal frames twisted, and the shed door has been ripped off. I don't know when, but the anger has swept through.

I make my way to the back door and actually sigh with relief when I realize I have been gifted a way in. There are a couple of smashed window panels from the recent days and nights of violence.

Why is the glass on the outside, though? That means it was broken from the inside. Someone inside did this … to their own house?

I try the door handle and find it locked, however, I can see that the keys are still hanging in the barrel on the inside. I reach through and turn them, being careful not to cut myself on the broken glass.

I was familiar with Amy's flat, familiar with the layout and confident in my surroundings. It was my small world that only consisted of five rooms and a straight hallway. This is a new and dangerous world, a veritable maze with too many undiscovered corners, rooms, and points of entry.

I walk through the medium-sized kitchen, find myself in the lounge, and my stomach pulses with a deep anxiety. A part of me still wanted this to be a mistake. A part of me still wanted the baby's cries to be a result of my imagination.

I see a changing table with a box of nappies stacked on its left side. I see a play mat with soft butterflies hanging off of it. I stare, as my eyes drop a few tears, at a photograph of the baby, taken at birth, on the coffee table.

Carter Sebastian.
11.08.17
7lb 9oz

This is real. This is so fucking real! You weren't imagining it. There is a baby here, Carter Sebastian, and you have no choice but to accept it … accept him. You have to accept this future … this story.

I have a few friends with children, and all their faces start to fly through my mind at high speed, relentlessly trying to help. The closest by far is Tammie. I focus my thoughts on her, recalling all the times we've chatted or had a cup of tea together, and I realize that she has taught me a lot, without even trying to. She also helped me, so very much, after I broke up with Darius, my last boyfriend.

Darius … you hurt me. Your words really hurt me. I know they were said in panic, and you didn't have a chance to think them through properly, but that's why they were so painful. They were said instinctively.

Tammie has four boys and is a true Supermum if there ever was one. I've seen all of her children grow up, the eldest now being eleven. She lives down the road from me and my mum, and we've all become close over the years, since I was a teenager.

Although the lounge here has items dotted about for the new baby, I can see the style has been set by a home loving perfectionist. I've met many of those in my time. A tidy home is a happy home, a place for everything and everything in its place.

I walk through, guessing there will be stairs up ahead, admiring the décor as I go. The neat lines, the mahogany furniture, the maroon walls, they all inspire a much welcomed calm within.

"Ggeelllaagelllagguh!"

I hear the random sound close by … *he's upstairs …* and bolt towards it.

I'm here! I'm here now!

The stairs are to the left at the end of the lounge. I try to ignore the scene outside the window as I dart up, two stairs at a time.

"Where are you, baby boy? Carter?" I say in a playful and raised tone, unsure where he actually is. There are four doors off of the landing, none with any clear indication for me to follow.

Try them all!

I grab the first handle. Bathroom. The second is a double bedroom, however, it looks untouched and without any 'life'.

Spare bedroom?

I open the third door and am shocked by what I see, enough to stop moving for a second. The window has been blocked up by cushions, pillows, and a rolled up duvet. The walls have thick curtains attached to them with lines of random duct tape, and there are also a couple of rugs rolled up on top of piles of clothes as well.

I step in and see a rainbow coloured teddy bear on the floor, a long caterpillar of the same colours perched up on another pile of clothes, a fluffy elephant with blue stars on it, and a blue owl with lights glowing from inside.

"Uuhhoooooh."

I turn to my left and my heart pumps as I see him, sitting in a bouncer chair, staring around the room, oblivious to any of the horrors outside.

"Hi, baby," I say. "Hi, Carter."

Carter looks directly at me and smiles. His head wiggles from side to side, his arms shoot out, and his legs kick as if he is running a race. He looks so different to the photograph downstairs, despite the short amount of time that has passed. His hair is darker and much thicker on top, styled into a spiky mohawk by all his fidgeting. The radiant eyes are wide and sparkling, plus there are perfectly rounded, peach shaped cheeks.

"I'm here," I say, and pause for a second, lost entirely in the moment. "My name is … is Shayla. You … you look like a happy little one. Are you? Are you a happy little boy?"

I'm replied with a smile, a sneeze, Carter poking his tongue out at me, and another sporadic dash of the legs.

Mum? Mum? What do I do? Help me … please?

Chapter nine

Tammie is an organised parent, although she won't admit this to anyone, not ever. I've come to think that she believes the opposite, which is utterly ridiculous, and an unnecessary attack on her self-esteem. She apologized to me quite a few times because her house was untidy when I visited. It wasn't untidy. It was as clean as it could be, neat, with four boys living inside it, one of them only seven months old. There's a huge difference, trust me. She cooked me amazing meals, yet wouldn't accept the praise they deserved, and said sorry that she 'almost' forgot my birthday one year. She didn't forget it, so there wasn't any need to feel that way in the first place.

Tammie has told me in the past, usually after I've asked 'How do you manage all of this so well?', that she lives by a strict set of lists, ones that exist inside her Supermum head. Her fiancé, Jayce, runs his own business, so his working hours are often long and random. It was a simple choice for Tammie to devote her life to the children and the family home. I know she has already planned to go back to college. She wants to gain the qualifications needed to work in schools as a teaching assistant.

I hope you're all still out there, somewhere. You are all safe and looking to the future.

It never worried Tammie that her plans are four or five years away. Her youngest, Thomas, will begin full time education then, and she won't be 'needed' as much. They were set, and they weren't going to change. She wanted to carry on helping children, bringing them up, and teaching them in whichever way she could.

Tammie's lists were quite extensive, and she seemed to have one for every situation, or occasion. They came with years of practise, I suppose, and the crucial lessons learnt with every day as a parent. There was the daily mum routine, the daily fiancée routine, and the daily keep-the-house-in-order routine. On top of all that, she had to think about the shopping, the school run for the morning, the school run for the afternoon, what shall we all have for dinner tonight?, *and,* these-things-will-run-out-soon-so-I-better-pick-them-up.

Supermum. Super person. Super friend.

She saw me walking back to my house after I split with Darius. I wasn't crying, I'd hidden the tears away by then, however, she knew I was upset. She saw through me and sensed that something was wrong.

'Come on, let's go and sit in the back garden and I'll make you a tea,' she said.

We did exactly that. We sat in her garden, drinking tea in the sunshine, talking about Darius. Perhaps it was a maternal superpower, I don't know, but she seemed to guess that it had something to do with motherhood. Only perfectly timed and worded questions followed from her lips. Every facial expression was coated with care and understanding.

A few hours earlier, I'd told Darius how I'd seen a few large spots of blood in the toilet. I had also known my period was late for close to two weeks. I knew what had happened. It was one of the strangest moments in my life as well. In only a few crucial seconds, the world was taken from me, a new world, before I'd even had a chance to live in it.

Darius, you turned on me so quickly. You changed in the blink of an eye.

My words, my genuine apologies, were coated with equal measures of anxiety, sadness, and worthlessness. His immediate reaction was less than positive. I wanted him to rush forward and grab me in his arms, however, he stayed on the other side of the room, and fell silent. He asked me too many questions about the 'protection percentage guarantee' of condoms.

He fell silent again. Then, he mumbled a lot. He shouted at me because I'd lied and kept important secrets from him. I'd been devious and self-centred.

It all fell apart, Darius. It should have made us stronger … it should have been us against the sorrow and shock … not you turning against me …

He listed off quite a few reasons why we *couldn't*, and *shouldn't*, be parents. I say we, but that's actually a mistake, there were far more reasons why *I* couldn't and shouldn't. Many of those, if not all, hurt me.

With little effort it seemed, Darius managed to twist trivial facts around to insinuate how I would be a bad mother. I liked a brandy at the weekend, I forgot my door keys on occasion, or let my washing build up.

No, Darius. No. Why do that? It really fucking hurt. Why didn't you just admit that you were upset, like I was? Be angry, but not at me! Why did you have to say those things?

'Hey, listen to me, Shayla, please. My kids have grown up with you in their lives. They all love you, okay? Remember that. You'll be a great mum one day, I know it.'

Thank you, Tammie.

The list I am reading through now, in my overstretched memory, is the 'why-is-the-baby-crying?' list. It's one I'm going to need to remember.

Does he need his nappy changed? Is he hungry? Tired? Too hot, or too cold? Does the baby need some attention, or comfort? Is there pain due to teething, or a stomach ache?

I've seen Tammie do exactly the same and work her way through the questions, firsthand.

From physical appearance, and his behaviour, Carter appears to be fine at the moment. He hasn't cried since I've arrived, yet I have no way of knowing when he last fed, or slept.

Don't panic, Shayla. You can't panic, you can't!

"You want your nappy changed? Yeah? Shall we get you all clean? Yeah, that's a good place to start."

Carter smiles at me, sticks his tongue out several times, snorts, and kicks his little legs with excitement.

You're so … so …

I have no choice but to take a deep breath to settle my emotions. Carter's deep eyes, yet to fully find their colour, bore through me. They are a magical blue and golden mix at the moment. I have a strong feeling they will be brown soon, just like mine.

You're the most precious little man I have ever seen. I promise I'll look after you … I'll do whatever I can …

"Carter, do you want to come for a walk with me? Yeah, that sounds fun, doesn't it? Let's go downstairs and make sure I know where all your stuff is."

Carter's eyelids drop as I speak. He's staring at me, but getting ready to sleep. I decide to leave him here, comfortable and surrounded by his familiar toys.

I see a light-blue dummy by the side of the chair, so place it gently in his mouth. "I'll be back to change you in a minute, okay, little man?" I whisper as I lay my forefinger in Carter's miniscule palm.

••

I check through the lounge and place all the essential items I find there on the burgundy sofa. I haven't thought about how I will travel home with Carter, a box of nappies, several sets of clothes, plus the other items I've managed to grab as well. My memory assures me there is a pram folded up in the kitchen.

This stuff isn't going to last forever. What do I do when it runs out?

I try to imagine myself walking through the streets

around here, and Rayleigh's main town, picturing all the shops close by.

If it's truly deserted, if the people have all gone, how does it work out there now? Do I just walk inside the shops and take whatever I want off of the shelves?

I open all the cupboard doors in the kitchen to make my search easier. I realize I am moving about in a frantic state, flitting from one side of the room to the other. My behaviour is strange, slightly erratic, but I don't care, nor try to stop it from happening.

This is like a first-aid cabinet ... indigestion medicine, cough syrup ... Ah, excellent, there are bandages. I need to strap this wrist up.

I gently cover my swollen wrist and pull the bandage as tight as I can. It hurts from my palm to near the elbow, and I have to grit my teeth on more than one occasion.

"Milk powder ... bottles ... that's all we need," I say, wondering immediately when 'I' became 'we'.

My mind halts for a moment as Darius' face appears. It is exactly the same expression he wore when he was immersed in his verbal tirade. He split the plural, *our plural*, to a single, and I have rebuilt it, albeit with Carter.

I push Darius' image out of my head, replacing it with Carter's eyes, his heart-melting grin, and I can't help but smile myself. *You're proving Darius wrong. You're fighting back against his cruel and unnecessary words.*

A chilled breeze punches through the smashed windows in the kitchen and I see a terrible contrast, a positive against a startling negative. Carter is safe upstairs, surrounded by warmth and soundproofed to the best of his mother's ability. This kitchen is icy-cold, though, wide open, almost calling the anger inside. I don't trust myself or my limited skills to repair it before sunset.

I take the milk powder and bottles to the lounge and sit down, trying to think. It is so difficult to plan ahead when I have no idea what will be there. It is like walking down a dark alleyway when you are unsure of where it might lead, or what

61

awaits you at the end.

My eyes notice a patch of red on the changing bag to my right, and it sparks a memory. I can't remember if I learnt it from Tammie, or the other parents I socialize with, yet I know there will be a red book in this house somewhere. I am one hundred percent certain of this fact because all children have them. They contain basic health information, growth charts, and immunisation dates. It won't help me now, it won't help me in the next minute, hour, or day, but it will be great to find. I can't describe the feeling pushing through me. It's an eagerness, an urge, to know that Carter is healthy, that he is well.

I know you don't want to … I know you don't want to think about it right now, but you have to. It isn't safe here, it doesn't feel secure enough, like Amy's did. We can't go back, though, we have to keep moving forward.

The train station is approximately ten minutes away from here, and there are many houses along the road, however, I can't know if they will be any safer than this one. Fear and uncertainty are dancing around me, and I am unable to clear my mind long enough to make a solid choice.

Chapter ten

After sneaking back upstairs, so I could change Carter's nappy, I came back to the lounge and sat down. He slept peacefully through the whole process, and was completely quiet as well. I was even given a few smiles from his adorable little face. They are completely contagious and I cannot stop myself from joining him.

It is nine o'clock. I should be thinking about a thousand other things, however, I am smoking one of the mother's cigarettes that I found in the kitchen. I used to smoke, quit four years ago, so I'm not sure what this will do for me. A part of my mind is telling me it will help with the stress, however, there isn't any. I'm scared by this as much as I am by everything else.

I spent the entire night in distress, dealing with terror I couldn't have believed possible, yet now, for an unknown reason, I am completely calm. I should be a wreck, I should be drowning in the pool of blood. It could be because of Carter, or it could be the beginning of an acceptance towards the situation. I can't believe either, although it has to be a possible eventuality. One morning, I will wake up and believe what has happened to the world, and to my life, even if I still do not have any answers.

Or, your mind will break, Shayla. You'll dive willingly towards the congealed blood, without hesitation. You'll be at peace there ... at peace.

I fear so much for Carter's safety, and I am nowhere near to accepting that the world changed in a matter of days. There will also be a sunset every evening, so my new fear will never cease to attack me once the sun goes down. The thought of it is enough to send a lightning bolt of panic and nausea through my body. If this is my 'calm before the storm' moment, if this is a short period of inner peace while my mind and body find themselves within the chaos, what will happen to me when the storm, *my storm*, hits?

How far away is home?

I stand up and grab the tablet computer off of the dining table. As I type my postcode in the search bar, I stare out of by the back windows and, unfortunately, remember the sight of the dead dog very close by.

A map appears, as well as several links to local businesses, telling me it is approximately seven miles away. The numbers differ slightly depending on which method of travel I choose.

"I know I can't drive legally, but I *can* drive."

I think about my words, then imagine myself taking car keys from any house I choose. My eyes flick a glance behind me, out of the lounge window. I can see a black car on the driveway, although I'm unsure of its manufacturer.

No, think of Carter … you must always make the right choice, the safest one …

I also think about the state of the roads that I have seen so far. They are littered with abandoned vehicles, as well as smashed up brick walls, lamp posts, and mounds of rubbish. It would probably take me a lot longer than it should if I was in a car.

I turn back to the dining table. I was going to look at the pile of letters on top, but I see a handbag on one of the chair seats.

A moment of morality follows, pushed away as quickly as it arrived. I need answers, clues, *anything*. I've decided with ease that I feel no regrets about searching through this handbag, this house … *any* handbag or house.

Apart from the purse and mobile phone, it is full of the usual clutter that only a woman would understand as necessary.

I push the power button on the mobile and the home screen appears. There doesn't seem to be a security pin in place, so I tap through to the messages app. My other hand rakes out bank cards and anything else that looks useful from the purse.

"Your name is … Susan Heath," I say, reading the embossed letters from a credit card.

A train pass, one with a photograph, drops out of the purse and falls on the table. Susan looks to be in her mid-thirties, with long and wavy black hair. Her brown eyes seem loving, calm, and wise beyond her age.

Is that why Carter feels safe with me? Is it because my eyes are the same colour as his mum's?

I turn my attention to the mobile phone. "Mark from work, someone called Sylvia, and …"

My eyes suddenly focus when I see the date of the message.

Sunday morning? That's the most recent of anything I've found so far!

I tap the screen again before I realise that I'm holding my breath, and my fingers are trembling.

Samuel, brother (Mob)

I've been trying to phone you, but I think there's something wrong with the networks. Are you two, and Carter, okay? I've had messages all night long from people saying there is trouble near you as well! It's everywhere!

Sunday, 07:14

Sam! Thank goodness you're safe! I was so

scared. I can't reach Callum, he's not answering
calls or texts. I've been hiding upstairs with Carter
through the night.

Sunday, 07:17

Who is Callum? I think. *I suppose he is Susan's boyfriend, or
husband, and Carter's dad?*

I scan the room very quickly and find a photograph
on the fireplace mantle. Susan, Carter in her arms, and a
man with light-brown hair and a caring smile.

The police have told everyone to stay indoors, lock
everything up, and keep quiet. Why do we need to
be quiet?

Sunday, 07:18

I don't know. I'm so scared, Sam! I heard
terrible screams during the night.

Sunday, 07:20

My friend from work sent me this video last night. I
really don't know what to believe. People have told
me messed up stories. Sickening stuff.

Sunday, 07:21

Watch it in a minute. Read the rest of the messages first, I
think as my thumb hovers over the screen, desperate to touch
the play icon.

What was that??

Sunday, 07:24

I don't know! I can't make sense of any of this.

Sunday, 07:26

Sam, can you get down here? Just jump in
your car and drive! Please!

I'll try and find out what's happening, and also get some help. I'll text you back as soon as I know more.
Sunday, 07:29

Hurry, please!

Sunday, 07:30

Love you. Tell Carter that Uncle Samuel loves him.
Sunday, 07:31

Love you.

Sunday, 07:31

There are no more messages in the conversation. Samuel and Susan never spoke to each other again, at least not through text messages. My heart is warmed by the fact they parted with love, and broken because I never had the same with my mum.

She knows, Shayla, she knows. Tell her when you get home. Throw your arms around her and shout it out loud. WHEN YOU GET HOME!

"Samuel said there were problems with the phone networks in his messages. Perhaps that's why I haven't been able to reach Mum?"

I mumble the words only to myself. They are powered along with a glimmer of hope that pumps at my heart.

When I first received the voice messages on my phone from Mum, when all this began, I allowed horrific and soul crushing imagery inside my mind. Now, although I still feel guilt beyond measure, I have started to replace it with traces of positivity. I tell myself that Mum is hidden in our house, much as I was in Amy's. It works for one minute in every couple of hours.

I scroll back to the video in the message and my thumb hovers again. I stare, in a kind of trance, at the play

67

icon, the white triangle that could possibly bring forth a vital clue.

I don't want to see this. I do want to see this. I don't want to see this.

I've desperately needed to find answers ever since I ran out of the door at Amy's, and yearned to understand. Now, as I stand here, gifted with a possible reason, I freeze, unwilling to accept it. I don't want to watch. *I do want to watch … I do.*

I touch the screen, unable to control the instinctive snap of movement, and the video begins to play.

There's a normal house on the left of the screen, but the camera focuses more on the garage door. It's made from grey metal panels and I guess they either lift up, or move on an automated roller.

"I don't know what's going on," begins a male voice, the one recording the video. The tone is blatantly terrified. "I saw her run inside a few hour ago, just before six. I've tried to call the police, but there's no answer! I keep getting the same recorded message, the one about staying indoors."

The male moves the camera closer to the garage door, taking slow steps. He's a few metres away and I can hear his cracked and shuddering breaths.

"Sirens were blasting all night long, and I haven't been able to sleep much … I couldn't."

I hear a noise on the video, like metal being slowly scraped.

"Can you hear that?" asks the male. "Is the camera picking that up?"

I flinch and jolt on the spot when a roar immediately follows. It sounds like a caged animal has suddenly realized it is caught, *and* ultimately trapped.

"Whoa!" cries the male. The video zooms out suddenly as he back steps away from the garage for safety.

Get away from there! Run! RUN! I think. I'm right back

68

on the flip-side of the horror movie again, screaming at the screen, deciding that the protagonist is a naïve moron, soon to die.

Whatever is inside the garage roars once again, then growls with a sadistic edge. It is beyond evil, unlike anything I've heard before. The passionate undertone has returned as well, the one I heard during the night at Amy's. It *wants* to feel this rage, it is gaining some sort of sadistic pleasure from its own dark feelings.

I flinch again when a loud bang on the garage door surprises me. The metal panels shake in rapid succession.

"Shhiiitt!" says the male voice, drawn out on a breath.

More bangs follow at an impossible speed, so fast they almost become one continuous blast. The panels start to buckle and dent in large areas, the roars grow louder, and the video ends.

I drop the mobile phone on the table. *My storm is coming and I feel powerless. I can sense it close by.*

Carter makes a beautiful squeal upstairs as he wakes from his nap.

The baby ...

It carries through the house, as if made of pure sunlight, fighting away the thick clouds in my mind, battling my fears head on.

"Carter ... I'm here, Carter. Don't worry, baby," I whisper.

Chapter eleven

Susan has quite a few bottles of baby formula in the kitchen, ones that are sold ready for use. I pour one out into a sterilized bottle, then take it upstairs for Carter.

I checked the tin of powdered milk before I left the lounge, just to see how much a child of his age should be having. It is one area of caring for a baby that I am going to have to learn all on my own. I can't bring a memory into my mind to give me the definitive answer.

"Hi, Carter. I've brought you some breakfast!" I say as I hold the bottle out in front of me.

I sit down next to him, being careful not to lean too much on my wrist. He smiles widely and kicks with excitement.

I need some painkillers, and ibuprofen as well. I'm sure I saw some of them in the cupboard downstairs.

Fortunately, it's comfortable for me here with all the pillows, blankets, and clothes on the floor.

I pick Carter up and he settles in my arms without hesitation, almost diving his lips towards the bottle.

"What shall we do now? Any ideas?" I ask.

Carter is too busy feeding to make a sound. He does stare at me, though, his eyes fixed on mine.

Be careful. He doesn't recognise you, remember? All his trust could disappear very quickly.

"I know this is your house, and your mummy did a

fantastic job of keeping you safe, she really did, but I don't think we can stay here. We have to keep moving, Carter. We have to keep going, do you understand? I don't want to stop, not yet," I explain in a soft and steady tone of voice.

"You have a lot of archways downstairs in your house. If there were doors, I might have been able to make it safer for us both, like I did at my friend's."

Could I do it, though? Could I move the furniture again and make it secure enough here?

I take the half-full bottle away and sit Carter up on my knee. He screams at me as I gently tap and rub his back.

"Oh, no, don't cry … you're fine, it's all good …"

Carter straightens his body, turns his head, then burps loudly in my face.

"Oh! Good boy! Good boy!"

A short cry follows, plus a cute scrunched up face. I have a feeling that I can work out the translation.

'I gave you exactly what you wanted. I burped for you, young lady. Now, kindly put the bottle back in my mouth, I'm still hungry.'

You have no idea how much you have saved me. You're looking after me as much as I am you …

I carry on feeding Carter as I think about the immediate future. It's obvious to me, and it's so strong a thought I physically feel it as a burst of anxiety, that we can't stay in this house. It's close to ten o'clock, so we have just over six hours of daylight left before I'm expecting *their* return. I have no idea what my enemy even is, yet I fear them with unwavering conviction.

"How long were you here?" I ask Carter. He's staring again, thoroughly enjoying his breakfast.

His mum couldn't have left that long ago. Babies need to feed every few hours, sometimes even sooner.

The thoughts create questions, and I can't answer any of them. For all I know, I could have missed Susan by minutes, or a couple of hours.

But ... why leave him here? What made her do that? She created this room for him, for his safety, then left. It doesn't make any sense!

I sit Carter up again and he makes an extended 'Ooooh' sound at me. His tiny hand brushes against my finger, and I let a few tears fall.

••

I changed Carter's clothes for a maroon onesie with the Hogwarts crest on the front, a pair of black jogging bottoms, and a knitted white cardigan.

A gorgeous streak of November sun has punched through the clouds in the sky, however, the smashed windows in the kitchen are allowing chilled air to flow around the house, especially the lounge.

"Carter, does your mummy have a printer?" I ask. He's in my arms as we walk around the lounge. "I might print out a map of the different routes to my house."

I can't see one, which I find unusual, so I just grab the tablet computer and try to focus my concentration. *I need to get to the town, then ... then I'll go straight down Eastwood Road and Rayleigh Road. I can head towards Leigh-on-Sea from there, by the woods ...*

"I know people down there, Carter. We have friends, places to rest and hide."

"Aayyoooo."

I giggle at the reply, well, Carter's version of one.

If they're ... if they're still alive ... I shake my head and grit my teeth to send the thought away.

Susan's handbag is in front of me on the dining table, and I notice a set of keys inside. There's only two on the keyring, and it has a blue plastic tag attached as well.

"Angela. 17."

An immediate and loud idea shouts at me. "Come on, Carter. I need to check on something."

I walk towards the front windows and take a look outside. I haven't heard any roars or growls since I arrived here, not close by, nor in the distance.

No, don't go out there unarmed.

I grab the meat cleaver out of my rucksack, keeping it covered with the tea-towel, and shove it between my back and the waist of my jeans.

I slowly open the front door and see I am in number nineteen. If my idea was correct, I have the keys to the neighbouring house, to Angela's.

I walk down the path, my eyes darting left and right, my ears listening for any sounds at all. I'm not far from Amy's and my eyes have no choice but to stare down the road. I see a shape on the floor, I deliberately searched it out if I'm truthful. The dead body ... the dead woman. I turn my head and notice some smoke drifting from the roof of a house further towards the train station. Every car in my line of sight is either tipped over, covered in dents, or has smashed windows. One of them, a maroon SUV about three houses away, is missing the roof, ripped completely off and thrown on the road.

I think of Samuel's video message. The strength I witnessed, hidden and brutal, behind the garage doors.

Hurry up! Check the keys ... come on!

I hold Carter close to me and pull the hood up on his cardigan. Despite the sun, it feels crisp in the air, like a tingling layer of skin. Fortunately, the breeze has a cleansing aroma, not the stench I had expected.

I reach the door of number seventeen and manage to get the keys in without fumbling around, as I did at Amy's.

"Yes! I was right!"

Carter jumps slightly in my arms, then spits his dummy out. "Oh, sorry, baby, sorry," I whisper.

I walk inside and close the door behind me. "If this place is safe, we'll stay here for a while, okay? We'll stay here and move again as soon as we're ready."

Carter makes a snorting noise and wobbles his head about.

"Nnnngooo."

I think he agrees with me.

Chapter twelve

Angela, I love this place … and I think I love you a little bit as well.

Within a couple of seconds of walking through the front door, I already know this house is going to be so much safer than Susan's. It appears more closed in, separated from the outside world, and warmer as well.

I'm enclosed in a dark, and very small, entrance area. It is decorated with uncovered bricks, patches of beige plasterwork, and some sepia photographs. The staircase ahead of me has been created from varnished wood, and it manages to produce beauty and fear in one gothic moment.

Angela, I do love you. For this staircase alone, I love you.

"I really don't want to jinx it, Carter," I say, "but this is almost perfect. It is exactly what we need."

We walk towards the lounge and, because the curtains are closed, I flick on a light. There's a strip of material running down the door's edge, and I recognise it from my own house. It is used to extend fire resistance, which means the door is made of thick wood, and it serves to add immediate weight to my feelings of security. A thick door equals precious seconds of time to hide, or escape from any danger.

When did I start to think this way? When did I become a … what am I? A survivor? I think, trying to pinpoint the exact moment. It had to be while I was at Amy's, although much of my time there, especially after I listened to Mum's messages, is a blurred mess of dreadful memories.

Carter's eyelids keep slowly dropping as he prepares to take another nap. I don't want to leave him, to ever let him go, yet I want to investigate my new surroundings. *I want to investigate my new surroundings … with a powerful meat cleaver held firmly in my hand.*

I grab a couple of thick cushions from the armchair to my right, then place them behind it on the floor. It isn't perfect for Carter, but it will do for now. He will be comfortable because they are so soft, hidden if necessary, and protected, even if it is only with a piece of furniture.

"If your mum has a set of keys to this house, I expect you've been here a few times," I whisper. "If you do wake up, I promise I won't be far away. I want to make sure we are safe here, okay?"

I smile as I look at Angela's decorative style in the lounge. My eyes find thick rugs on the floor, old-fashioned wooden trunks stacked by the beige sofa, *and,* an upright piano.

That will make a great barrier. I should be able to move it, so it blocks one of the doorways.

My joy and excitement make me wonder how many times I have smiled since meeting Carter. I can't remember if I did it at all while hiding at Amy's. I certainly didn't have any need to.

Finding Mum at home, probably shut inside her bedroom, scared but unharmed, plus keeping Carter safe and content … they are my reasons to smile now. They are my only reasons.

I look at the piano again, think of a few other musical instruments, and then, strangely, Joanna, a very unexpected face. She is a wonderful musician, also a book lover, and a good friend, even though we don't get to see each other that often. We met at the wedding of our mutual friend, Jasmine, about two years ago. I'll never forget how she ended up playing a few pieces of music at the reception. One of them, a classical composition, made the bride shed a few tears of happiness.

I walk towards the back of the house, through the door to the kitchen, and see double-glazed windows, all intact. The anger seems to have ignored here, left it unsullied and in peace. It is like a building that, somehow, defies all logic and the laws of physics to survive through an earthquake.

Oh, she's away on holiday. Is that why? No sounds to entice them in, no lights, or movement? I wonder as I read the calender stuck on the fridge door. It has a line running through last week and this one, with words scribbled along it. *'Away with Matthew in Ireland'.*

Are you safe, Angela? Has all this spread to other countries as well?

Charlie's voice appears inside my head. 'If it has, *how* is it doing so?'

I add a new entry to my 'what is happening' list, and it is quite random. *A virus? Some sort of illness? A scientist went out last week, got blind drunk, then dropped a test tube the next day? This is all because of a fucking hangover?!*

Being in the kitchen brings my dry mouth and cramped stomach all the more to the forefront of my thoughts. I left my rucksack next door, so walk towards the fridge to check for food and drink. I can't possibly look after Carter if I am not aware of, and in control of, my own health. I'm functioning, although I know I am constantly on edge, nauseous, and my head is clouded with confusion.

There isn't much in here, or in the fruit bowl to my right on the worktop. I suppose Angela didn't shop very much because of her planned holiday.

"Lemonade … bottled water … that's about it," I mumble.

The cupboard isn't much better, however, there are tins of food, as well as biscuits and crackers. I grab both packets, return to the fridge for some butter, and prepare a small snack.

As I sip at the bottled water, I reach for one of the apples and squeeze it. I'm satisfied it is ripe and fine to eat, so take a large bite.

I need the rucksack ... and Carter's stuff is still next door as well.

I decide to run back to Susan's so I can start moving everything between the two houses.

Wait! What about Carter?

A few minutes of harsh indecision follow. I don't want to leave him, yet I tell myself he is safe indoors.

Just go. It will take a few minutes, nothing more. No ... no. You have to stay with him ... you have to ...

I argue some more with my own thoughts, then reach a compromise. I will grab the rucksack, a few essentials, then take Carter with me for the rest later on, when he is awake again.

I walk back through the lounge, check behind the armchair, then hurry out of Angela's house.

I've only walked a few steps along the street when I see something ... I see *someone.*

I am not alone out here.

Chapter thirteen

What ... do ... I do? HELP ME! WHAT DO I DO?

I know there will be no answer. I know the only voice I'll hear in reply is my own.

I can no longer even distinguish the individual beats of my heart, such are their incredible speed and ferocity. My legs try to stay steady, and I know I'm holding my breath, even though it is the most dangerous reaction. I need to breathe.

BREATHE! PLEASE!

My nostrils flare, my mouth opens wide, and I draw in a mighty gasp of air. The street moves and blurs, just for a few seconds, as I regain some essence of composure and control over my body. The fingers on my hand sting because they're grasping the wall to my left so tightly, yet I can't remember even reaching for it in the first place.

Across the road, under the shadows of a house wall, stands a young woman. She is sideways to me and her eyes are shut. They look strange, though, perhaps because of my angle of sight. The skin appears to be blurred, or even scarred, across the lower lid.

There is something so unsettling about this ... about her. She looks normal, about my age, with long blonde hair. Despite the chilled November air, she is only wearing a light-grey t-shirt, jeans, and sandals.

Get ... get back to Carter! Get back inside!

I can't move. I can't even create a thought to move any part of my body. I am paralysed with fear.

Breathe!

I do not breathe.

Move your legs. Take one simple step backwards.

I do not move my legs. I do not take one simple step backwards.

Why ... why isn't this working? Come on, please! COME ON!

I believe that my hand is creeping towards my lower back, albeit at an agonising pace. My fingers are totally numb and have no sense of touch, however, patches of my skin also feel frozen, and others are too hot and pouring with sweat.

My forefinger pushes against something near my spine, the handle of the cleaver, and it grants me enough confidence to move my leg. I feel a terrible sensation through my hand as it momentarily returns to life. It is as if I have just shut my fingers in a door.

The pain I suffered in my knee yesterday stabs at me, reignited by my awkward and disoriented movements.

Why isn't she moving? What's wrong with her?

I manage another step as I grasp the cleaver's handle. I still can't feel anything properly, yet I know I am pushing my grasp and muscles beyond their limits.

I reach the gate at the end of Angela's garden path, thrilled that I didn't close it on the way out here. Every piece of information I have discovered so far points to silence being imperative. They hear everything ... and it creates the anger they feel.

Is she like the one in Samuel's video? Is she full of rage?

I walk at such a slow pace that it takes me another minute to reach the front door. My vision is clouded and my eyes have started to sting as well. I won't allow myself to blink, or stop staring at her.

The keys ... she will ... will hear them ... she will see me ...

My heart, my suffering heart that still beats at a

catastrophic pace, sinks with a sense of defeat.

No … NO! I can do it. I can get the door open without any sound. I can. I have to.

I try to pull the recent memory of walking through Angela's front door out of my mind. I need to know the exact sounds the keys made, the click of the lock, the movement of the hinges. I can't find anything, though, and it was only a short time ago. I will have to live second by second, moment by horrifying moment, with my full concentration on the silent and unmoving woman. She is a mathematical equation of terror. The sum of her behaviour creates a fear parallel to that which devoured me during the night at Amy's. Her eerie stance, how she is almost frozen in time, the closed eyes, plus her body draped in shadows. It all multiplies together, and equals this moment for me.

I turn my head, focus on the lock, then lift the keys with a silent purpose and direction. I hold my breath and check on the woman. No change. She is a living part of this new landscape, immovable, and I've classed her as an immediate threat. All I can hope for is that she is not a permanent figure, and I will stare across the road at some point in the future to find her gone.

I push the key in with the most intricate amount of pressure. It is a task that requires all my will and calmness, such is the severity of my nerves.

It's working … I can do this … I can …

My hand wants to ignore the delicate movements and rush the act, so I stop and take a breath.

Stay calm … stay calm …

I turn the key as far as it will go, gently push the door open, and hold myself together for a few more seconds.

Step inside … keys out … shut the door.

I drop to my knees, covered in a sticky layer of sweat, and hold my stomach. I feel sick again.

I crawl through to the lounge and look behind the armchair. Carter is still fast asleep, unaware, with a mischievous smile on his face.

••

I know I can't allow the fear to cripple me. Images appear in my head of the woman rushing across the road to attack us both, screaming in the same sickening way as the one I heard in Samuel's video. They grow more ghastly and violent as I let them run with unstoppable freedom.

I have to move Carter to another room, as far away from the woman as is possible inside this house.

Well? Come on, move! Move now!

Despite the urgency, I am motionless. I mirror the stagnant behaviour of my new enemy, my unexpected tormentor.

With the gentlest of touches, I slip my hands underneath Carter's lower back and head. He stirs for a second, but, crucially, stays asleep and quiet.

Stand up, slowly. Think of Carter, think of his safety. Snap out of it! You have to concentrate!

My eyes stare out of the lounge window as I get to my feet. *She* is still there.

I back out of the lounge, holding Carter in a protective embrace, a shield I didn't realise I had the power to create. I'm willing to protect him if she attacks, without any hesitation. I'll stand my ground and fight her to the death, if that is what it takes.

I will. I'll do it for him.

I feel my emotions at war with each other. I feel a spark of strength, and of darkness, one that I always try to avoid. It is hatred.

This part of me, usually controlled, stirs with a longing to be set free, to soar from within my body. Thankfully, it is still in a dormant stage, suppressed, yet I fear it could appear soon. It wants to confront her, shout questions at her face, push her so that she actually moves, and hold my cleaver with authority. I want this unknown female to fear me instead.

All the doors upstairs are open, so I choose the one at the end of the landing, furthest from the lounge. It's a single room, used to store more old-fashioned trunks, clothes on a portable rail, and even a folding bicycle.

Yeah, this will work.

The room opposite looks to be the main bedroom, so I grab the pillows, four of them, and throw them across the landing. They have the same scent as my nightshirt and it grants me a moment of peace, a millisecond to make myself whole and synchronized once again.

I arrange the pillows between two wooden trunks, a wall, and the clothes rail. I'm content it will provide enough comfort, and dull any noises Carter might make.

I rush back through to the opposite bedroom and find the woman across the street.

I'm standing between two contrasting entities. One I fear completely, do not understand, and hate, even though it is not in my nature. The other is a helpless child I have sworn to protect. He has brought out maternal responsibilities I didn't know existed inside me, strong yet natural, unexpected yet welcomed without regret.

Chapter fourteen

I hear an adorable noise, plus some other excited squeals, coming from behind me. Carter is awake and it sounds as if he is attempting to laugh.

I walk through to his temporary bedroom and grab him in my arms. He smiles and rubs at his face as we walk back across the landing, my thoughts firmly on whether or not he will stay quiet.

When did he last feed? It was about an hour ago, hour-and-a-half, so we should be okay for a while longer. Don't forget nappy changes as well … and do not lose the dummy!

I nod at my own suggestions, as if I'm being given advice by another version of myself. A calm, courageous, and organized one.

"Can you be quiet for me? Yeah?"

Carter frowns. It is undeniably cute, but I also hope it isn't an unspoken response. If a baby wants to make a lot of noise, express itself in the only way it can, there isn't usually much anyone can do about it.

We head downstairs to the lounge, check on the unmoving female, then, I have a sudden urge to scream at myself with disappointment. Carter's formula bottles are still in Susan's next door. All the items I sorted out for him are on her sofa.

How am I going to get back? I need that stuff!

I swiftly turn around and head towards the back door

in the kitchen. There are a couple of fence panels down, near the end of the lawn, but that's the only damage I can see.

That will take me straight back to Susan's! I think with a triumphant and vigorous jolt. Climbing over wouldn't be a major problem, yet I can't even imagine leaving Carter all alone again.

I give him a soft 'fist-bump', then unlock the back door. There are two keys, a security chain, plus a thick bolt as well. It makes me love Angela just a little bit more than I already do.

I wonder why she is so security conscious? I mean, there doesn't necessarily have to be a reason, she might just like to feel safe in her own home.

Our house was burgled in the past, about eight years ago. I arrived home from visiting a friend for the afternoon, only to find a police car parked outside. There were two officers indoors, my mum shaking and in tears, and my dad was walking with loud steps through the house, saying 'Fuck!' a lot.

It took Mum ages to feel safe again, to feel comfortable in her own home … well, all three of us.

Mum explained to me, usually through tears and a nervous voice, that it had made the place she loved 'dirty', and she felt violated. Her home wasn't the same any longer.

I didn't experience that exact reaction, yet I understood her. I was angry, although I forget how I reacted. I think I focused on helping Mum through the ordeal, so I locked all my emotions away.

Angela's garden has been landscaped and maintained to a very high standard. This doesn't surprise me at all, having seen the inside of her house. There's an atmosphere throughout, a freedom of spirit almost, that she lovingly created.

I wonder if you're the keen gardener, Angela? I think you are. I hope you are. You seem like a very natural person to me.

I try to enjoy the beauty in front of me. I want to

distance myself from the fear for a moment, lose myself in the late autumnal colours, yet I can't. I'm not *allowing myself* to do it.

You're wasting time!

My thoughts prove that I have … have already changed, *and* I'm not finished yet. I'm a different person. I'm a different Shayla. There is always an urgency within me, coating my bones tightly underneath my skin. My reactions are instant and impulsive, my senses heightened, and it is becoming the new normal for me.

"Do you see those, Carter?" I ask as I point to the back wall of the house.

"Gaaah," he replies in a quiet tone.

I smile and hold in a laugh. "Gaaah, indeed. They are security lights, and I'm very glad we have them here. It means we can see what's happening when it gets dark."

I look at the sky for a second, then back to Carter. "*If* we are still here, of course."

There is an alleyway to my left side. I peek around the corner of the house and see that it leads to a tall wooden gate. I really want to take a closer look and inspect the area further, yet I know it's impossible with Carter in my arms. *She* is probably still across the road, so I can't take any unnecessary risks.

I head to the fallen fence panels, slowly and quietly, and step over them. I haven't been away from Susan's for very long, yet it looks like a different house somehow.

"I suppose this will be a good time to move your stuff across, Carter. Who knows how long that freaky bi …," I say, stopping myself deliberately.

Don't swear! You'll teach the baby!

" … how long that freaky … erm … bingo … will be out there for, eh?"

Carter smiles back at me, as if he understood my dilemma perfectly.

A strange period of time follows, one that is rhythmic

86

and structured. I move between the two houses, check on the woman every time I am close to the front windows, and transfer every needed, or useful, item across to Angela's.

••

The time is twelve forty-five. I have fed and changed Carter, and we are now staring out of the upstairs window.

I need to stop looking at her ... yes, stop, just stop ... but ... I can't ...

The continuous sight of the woman has evolved for me. Her lack of movement, her chronic stance, it is chilling. It's the perfect example of a foreboding fear, of the anticipation of an upcoming dread. My imagination has been forced to create possibilities about what will happen when she does move. All the scenarios, every one of them, are violent, savage, and I can't quite believe my own mind was capable of producing them. I thought I was a peaceful person, I abhorred confrontation of any kind, however, these thoughts weren't placed inside my head.

I made them. I am capable of such an unnatural hatred.

I hear birdsong in the back garden. It returns me to the immediate world, and also reminds me of a previous train of thought. I'm not certain when I first had it, or why, but I pushed it to the back of my mind. It was frightening, bold, and ultimately dangerous. I wanted to make some noise on purpose, to see if there is a reaction. I need to know if the anger hears me.

If the woman stays where she is, I'll have no choice but to rest here tonight, with Carter, and start my journey home tomorrow morning.

Mum ... I'm trying ... I'm trying to get to you, I promise. I'm so sorry ...

"I need to do ... do *something*," I whisper.

'Shayla, I know you are trying your best. I know it.'

The voice isn't mine, yet it is recognised and so very

87

needed. My heart gorges itself on the sweet and gentle tones.

'Now, think. Always think first. Think. Think again. Act.'

I will. Thanks, Mum.

I take a deep breath and regain control. My theory immediately bursts through, bullying, punching, and barging its way out of my thoughts.

You just need a safe way to do it. No rash ideas, no danger.

I disappear inside an imaginary world of my own creation. I'm in a bar with Charlie, and we're talking about all the ways to carry out my plan successfully. We smile, look at a few guys, and laugh as only close friends can. She drinks wine and I sip at a brandy with a splash of Pepsi.

Time moves at a different pace there, completely detached from the real world. I've only been staring out of the bedroom window for a couple of minutes, however, I drank another brandy and chatted to Charlie for at least ten.

If you do go over the edge, if you can't escape the dark liquid, find a place like this. Disappear inside your own mind.

It is decided, eventually, that I will use a mobile phone. I can grab Susan's from next door easily enough. I know it is unlocked as well, and that means I can get to her number, so it will be perfect.

This idea terrifies me …

I'll throw it over the fence of the house on the other side of Susan's, then, as soon as I am in position, and Carter is asleep and safe, I'll call her. Hopefully, the woman across the road will hear the ringtone. I can study her reactions and behaviour. I might learn nothing. I might learn everything. At the moment, I just want her away from me. I want to know that we can leave here tomorrow morning.

'It should work,' says Charlie. She has a look in her eyes that I can't place. I think it's concern. 'I'm more interested in how this happened, though. Aren't you?'

'I suppose so. I haven't really thought about the big picture to be honest. I can't. I'm … living in the moment, you understand? It has to be this way.'

Charlie shakes her head as she finishes her glass of wine. 'I *am* talking about the moment, Shayla. What you do now influences the future. *Your future.* Whatever happened out there, it took hold of everyone. They are either like the woman across the street, the one in the garage on Samuel's phone … *or* the dead body outside Amy's.'

I stare at Charlie, trying to see where her scientific thoughts are going. She always has a specific look on her face while her mind is calculating, or searching, through possibilities.

'It started somewhere, Shayla. There had to be a source. I know that it is probably impossible to discover now, but think logically. After the beginning, to reach so many people in such a small amount of time, it had to spread. How did it spread? Has it finished yet?'

I think about my hungover scientist theory, but stop myself before I can take it any further. *Enough! ENOUGH!*

I snap out of my daydream, angry with myself. These are *my* darkest fears, now given substance and a voice. The questions will only grow louder and more frequent. I should never have set them free.

Chapter fifteen

Move! You stupid … FUCKING BITCH! Move! Do something! Open your eyes and MOVE! Do you want me to come out there? Do you want me to grab the cleaver and come out there? ANSWER ME!

Chapter sixteen

Please move. Please? Don't just stand there. Please ... I ... can't take it any longer. I don't understand ...

Chapter seventeen

My mind is unhinged, once again tortured, and longing for the pool of congealed blood. It believes I will find peace there, drowning in the darkness.

It is almost three o'clock, and my mannequin like companion has picked away at my sanity for the last few hours. I feel mentally drained, and, although she hasn't done anything, it has been the most terrifying of all my encounters so far.

No movement, no voice, no sign of life at all. I can't explain the power and hold she has over me, it is too difficult to find words. Maybe I feel as if I am sitting in front of a loaded gun? This weapon could fire at any second, without warning, and kill me. Like I just said, it is very difficult to explain.

Pull yourself back from the edge! Step back!

I've granted this stranger a level of power I don't know she even deserves, and put so much danger around her presence.

Step back ... slowly ...

I turn my head towards the pile of cushions on the floor inside the opposite room. *Carter. Help me. Hold my hand as I walk away from the edge, please.*

No movement. No high pitched noises.

Why aren't you helping? You always help me.

"Unless ...," I whisper.

My mind twists reasons together, and tangles the situation for its own benefit. I know I'm about to lie to myself, but I don't care. It is working. *I'll take it.*

I know what I need to do. I am strong enough to step back on my own. Carter knows this as well, and that's why he doesn't need to wake up and help me. He trusts me.

"It is true … believe yourself!" I whisper through clenched teeth.

With a reluctance, one that I ignore and defeat with my new found clarity, I begin to make a mental list of what I need to do next. I let my creative thoughts rearrange Angela's furniture, and the heavy items she owns, until her house is secure.

Sunset is close, and an indescribable fear is growing inside me. Anger will return soon.

Chapter eighteen

This won't take me long. I just need to remember what I did at Amy's. Try and remember …

Downstairs, starting in Angela's lounge, I set myself to work. I close the curtains and deliberately leave a narrow slit, only a few centimetres wide. I design it that way so I can still see the woman in the shadows.

I push the sofa and armchairs around, and hang the floor rug over the back windows. It's very heavy, but I manage it. The dining table is already next to them, so I just add the chairs on top as extra security.

When I go upstairs, I'll drag the piano towards the lounge door and squeeze through the gap. Or, shall I use it against the main front door instead?

I grab bottled water, another couple of apples that still look edible, and formula for Carter. I'll take all these to the main bedroom later on, when it gets dark.

I'm not sure what to do with the kitchen, now that I'm standing inside it. I can't use the dining table, as I did at Amy's, however, Angela's tumble drier is next to the door.

Yeah, yeah, they're not difficult to move.

I drag it a few feet across the floor, double check I have everything, and turn off the light. I'm covered in a grey and hazy blanket, created by the late November sky, and it causes my skin to crawl. There are an unknown number of imagined and invisible insects, all born of fear, trying to claw and bite their way out.

No! Get back in the lounge ... take a deep breath! It's all in your mind!

I listen to my screamed thoughts and pull myself back together, mentally at least. My skin is still tingling, though, and I want to claw at my arms, neck, and face to try and stop it.

Finish down here, then get upstairs. They're coming. It's nearly dark out there.

Chapter nineteen

Sunset arrived thirty minutes ago. "I'm fine. I'm fine," I whisper. I get the words out even though my teeth are grinding together. It's an anxious trait I've carried with me for most of my adult life.

Thirty minutes. You've managed thirty minutes. You've survived the darkness for half an hour.

I look at the clock on my phone's screen. It's plugged in and charging next to me on Angela's bed.

Sunset arrived thirty-one minutes ago. "I'm … I'm fine," I whisper again.

Thirty-one minutes. Thirty-one.

The anger is out there. I can hear it, roaring in the distance, moving around in the dark.

I can't see across the road as well as I could earlier, the woman has new shadows allying with her. The left side of her body is covered in the dull-white glow from a working streetlamp, though. I think her hand moved a few minutes ago, although I could have imagined it. I don't trust my view of the world since the sun disappeared below the rooftops. My fears have returned, and I know I am not ready for another night. I don't know if I ever will be.

Carter and I both ate a short time ago, just after I ran out of the kitchen. As I was giving him the bottle, he stared at me in a very specific way. It was almost as if he knew I needed to eat and drink as well, and reminded me to do so with just his eyes.

"I'm scared, Carter. I'm really scared," I say, avoiding eye contact. I really don't want to upset him with my petrified expression.

"Hnnna," moans Carter through his dummy.

"Yeah, okay, I'll try. I'll be brave for you, I will."

Carter smiles and wiggles his head. I smile in reply, and take a moment to contemplate our unusual relationship. I've realized the reaction between us is key to my survival, and I've known this, *and* been using it, since the beginning. If I was still alone, I couldn't imagine where I'd be. Would I have even found the courage needed to actually leave Amy's? Would I have made it further and be in a different house by now, closer to home?

Carter's eyes closed while I was thinking. I'll hold him for a while longer, and gain the strength he offers me. I'll soak in the warmth from his tiny body, and we'll fight the darkness together.

I wish I could thank you enough. I wish you could understand how important you are to me.

We managed to get back to his house just before dark, to grab his mum's mobile phone and throw it over a fence. With him in my arms, the kitchen wasn't allowed to be terrifying. I fought back against it, for his sake.

I also grabbed the tablet computer, and found Susan's landline telephone number. I'm backing up my plan, but I don't understand how this forward thinking attitude, this survival knowledge, is in my head. All those years of watching horror and suspense movies has finally paid off, right?

I look at the woman. I know it is the perfect opportunity to start my experiment, however, I don't find myself rushing away from the window, keen to find a result.

Carter mumbles an innocent sound in his sleep, and a sick roar flows through the air a second later. It's to my right, coming from somewhere up the road near the train station.

I stare at Carter's peaceful face, then to the shadows

across the street, caught between love and hate.

••

Judging by today's routine, Carter will feed at about seven o'clock this evening. That leaves me almost two hours to carry out my plan while he sleeps, as safely as I could make him, in the small room opposite.

My heart suddenly leaps with shock, terror, and an unusual sense of relief. I don't quite believe my eyes at first, and step back a couple of feet, wary of the next few moments in my life. The woman … she just moved.

I've been waiting so long for this moment, yet I have absolutely no idea what to do next. "Shit!" I whisper.

I honestly thought she would be there forever, holding Carter and me as prisoners inside this house.

Do … something! Anything! She actually fucking moved!

The woman slowly turned her head to the left, stared at Susan's house for a few seconds, then turned back. I couldn't see her eyes, so I don't know if they were finally open, or still shut. I thought that they were scarred earlier, or disfigured, and I really wanted to check them again. I need to know her face … the face of this random anger! *It's my right to know!*

I believe that I deserve some answers after what she has put me through today.

You need to call Susan's mobile phone! You need to call it and see what happens! NOW!

I grab my own phone and scroll through to Susan's mobile number, added as a new contact a few hours ago. The bathroom is at the end of the hallway, with the window already open enough so I can look out to the garden. I'll have to leave the lights off in there, though, to conceal my movements.

I walk to the landing and check on Carter. His dummy is moving ever so slightly up and down between his lips, and his chest fluctuates in a soft rhythm.

"You be a good boy, okay? Stay asleep, and stay quiet. Please, be quiet."

Please ... I can't think ... I can't let myself think about one of them hurting you.

Simply because I don't want them to, the cruel thoughts appear once again, brazen and defiant. I close my eyes, grit my teeth, and even hit the side of my own head. The German Shepherd I saw in one of the gardens this morning transforms in my memory. First, it is me, dead with some of my shoulder ripped off, then ... then it becomes Carter.

No! Get out, get out ... GET OUT!

I have no choice but to distract myself. The images are so appalling, so repulsive, they are actually making me feel sick.

I go back to the bedroom window and find the woman in the shadows. Now it's my turn to play games. It's my turn to torment and harass.

I tap my phone screen a couple of times, let my thumb stop for a millisecond, then, without enough courage, press the green phone icon.

No! I wasn't ready!

Indecision punches me in the stomach as my mobile phone carries on with its important task, regardless of my weakened mental and physical states.

Earlier, I set Susan's phone to play a loud alarm style ringtone, similar to the digital clock I heard while at Amy's. Carter smiled and half-laughed at me when I rushed to grab a pillow to dull the sound. I admit, it did look comical as I flailed about in his lounge.

Maybe Susan did something similar in the past? Maybe I reminded him of his mum?

My eyes fix on the woman, and I listen as well, hoping that she does something ... *anything*.

What the ... fuuu ...

She walks out of the shadows by a few steps, although I *still* can't see her properly, and a growl rumbles through her throat. The reaction was instant, and layered with what I can only describe as coordinated, prowling, movements. She is stalking the sound of the mobile phone, setting up her attack.

Carter, please stay asleep!

The woman's shoulders raise as she runs across the street towards Susan's, disappearing out of my line of sight. The loud shatter of breaking glass follows.

Where is she? What did she do, jump through the lounge window?

I hurry through to the bathroom with silent steps. I have bare feet again, I deliberately took my boots and socks off about half an hour ago.

I climb on and around the sink, and position myself on the windowsill. It's a slightly precarious move, and I have to concentrate fully so I don't lean too far back, or let go of the window frame. My injured wrist constantly pulls and stings as I hold tight.

My phone vibrates. The call to Susan ended automatically because there was no answer. I quickly pull myself forward to a safe place, take a breath, and press the screen again.

It's working ... come on!

From this unusual position, I can hear Susan's phone as it starts ringing, even though it is a couple of gardens away. The ringtone is joined, and overpowered, by a growl which makes me shudder, and it forces the hairs on my neck to stand up. I feel as if there is an animal, or some creature, existing all around me, ready to kill.

Glass smashes again and I remember Mum's messages.

There are a few loud bangs and some wood snapping. I think of my night at Amy's and the dog I heard barking.

The woman's shape rushes out of the house, doused in shadows and darkness, moving across the garden.

The phone suddenly stops ringing as the woman roars. It sounds … sounds pleasurable.

What … what are you? What the hell has happened to everyone? I think, at a loss for an explanation yet again.

I'm sure I see a fence panel buckle and snap in half, although the shadows at the end of the garden are deep and concealing.

She's gone! She's heading back down the street, towards Amy's flat.

I want to sigh with an immense and complete relief, one that I can feel rising as warmth through my body. I want to cry my eyes out in victory. I can't, though, I can't move. I'm unable to even think, or function at all.

I slip myself down off the windowsill, as if all the bones in my body have shattered. I am skin, muscle, and blood, with no internal solidity. I fall to my knees in the dark bathroom, stare at my shaking hands, and force myself to breathe.

I know it's coming back for me, the fear I can't overcome. The deep pool of blood that wishes to hunt me down and wrap me in its grasp. It covets my body, longing to feel me close.

Think of Carter! No! Fight back!

It is a futile reaction, I am just too weak after witnessing the woman's outburst of rage.

I crawl through to Carter, sound asleep, majestically unaware of his present life, and lie down on the thick arrangement of pillows around his tiny body.

So young, so innocent.

My face is only inches away from his, and I can smell his beautiful scent, feel the warmth of his skin radiating to mine.

Don't leave him! Don't leave him alone! Use him, like you've done before. Use him to fight it!

I don't want Carter to ever see me in this state, and I don't want to be like this while caring for him either. I

101

wouldn't trust myself to be capable.

I close my eyes, knowing that my feet are on the edge of the stone cliff. I have a short amount of time to find myself again, to step back, to resist and succeed where I have failed before.

Chapter twenty

As we cuddle after a feed and a clean nappy, I stare at Carter's beautiful eyes. *I think they already look a different colour than they did this morning, more brown.*

I haven't even been with him for twenty-four hours yet, but he seems so changed to me. Apart from the slight physical difference, I'm noticing more facial expressions, smiles, and his mannerisms as well.

"Aaaooo," gurgles Carter. He kicks about with excited jolts as he looks around the room.

Angela's clothes, the ones in here on the rail, are floral patterned, or bright coloured, in what I would call 'Bohemian Chic'. Again, I am not surprised by this part of her life. She certainly has a style, and a connection to the natural world, one which she genuinely feels. Carter most definitely improves. He can't take his eyes off of them.

I think I slept for an hour or so. There is a period of time filled only with the thick and viscous pool of blood. It was different this time, though, growing stronger. I could taste and smell it as well, rancid and decaying, like the air outside.

I fought to escape, swim out, gasp in a breath, yet my actions only worked when I thought of Carter, or Mum.

He keeps saving me, the same as Mum does. He keeps pulling me back to the real world, desperate to protect me as much as I am him.

Tammie's lessons taught me that, hopefully, Carter will not feed again until the morning, *if* he sleeps through.

Some babies do, some do not. He does give off a very content personality, despite being so very young. In our short amount of time together, he hasn't cried once, although that could be partly down to me. Due to our dangerous situation, our newly entwined lives, I've never let him moan too much, fearing what would happen.

The woman has gone. She did as expected and followed the sound of Susan's phone. It angered her just as I guessed it would. I ... we ... we can start home tomorrow morning. We can go home.

'Why, though?' asks Charlie's voice. 'What actually happened? Ask *all* the questions, Shayla.'

I don't offer a reply to the imaginary voice of my friend. I don't even try to think of one.

•

It's one o'clock in the morning. *What day is it now? It's ... erm ...*

My mind is an empty room, dark and void of anything.

Seriously? I haven't forgotten that ... have I?

I'm exhausted to the point of severe nausea, I have a crushing headache, and every part of my body is sore with fatigue. I am determined to work this out, though. I have to succeed with something so trivial and give myself a positive. I need it, especially as it's the middle of the night and I'm outnumbered by the anger, forced to hide away and listen constantly to their cries.

I fell ill on Friday evening ... yeah, it was Friday. I felt better on ... Tuesday morning. That's when this all started. So, it's now ... Thursday. Is it? Hold on, Tuesday stuck indoors at Amy's, Wednesday to Susan's and Angela's ... couldn't go anywhere because of the woman across the road. Yeah, it's early on Thursday morning.

As I congratulate myself, I realise I have my mobile next to me, with the date and time on the screen.

01:08. Thursday, 23rd of November.

104

I haven't got the energy to swear at my own stupidity, not even in my head.

This ridiculous act proves to me that I *need* to close my eyes. I know I have to grab every single second of genuine rest, yet I'm too scared to do so, even though I do feel safe here. I believe I have done enough for Carter as well. We are warm, and I have padded the small window with the duvet from Angela's bed. The curtains in here are made of a thick material, although I still have the door open, and there is a lamp on in the hallway. The anger disappears in daylight, that much I know. They don't act differently towards manmade light sources, though, not that I've witnessed. Half of the woman's body was covered by the streetlight earlier, and she didn't react to it. My vampire theories suddenly resurface, however, I am not interested in listening. I push them away just as quickly as they arrived.

Please ... relax now ... sleep ... I want to move away from here tomorrow. I need to move, to get home!

The chorus from the anger sings all around me as my eyelids drop and I start to drift away. I'm caught between fighting to stay awake and surrendering to sleep, stuttering on the crossroads of the real and dream worlds.

Am I asleep? Wake up! What time is it?

I grab my phone. 2:37.

No ... don't sleep ...

3:14.

You have to protect him ...

4:12.

Stay awake ... stay with him ...

5:51.

Suddenly, I am back at home, sitting in the kitchen. Mum is here with me, drinking tea as she always does, and Carter is mumbling nonsensical baby words to us both from his highchair. He's smiling and banging his hands on the tray in front of him with excitement.

So, I finally gave in and fell asleep? This is a dream, I know it

105

is ... and I don't care. I don't want to wake up, not yet. This is exactly what I want, my ultimate wish, so I'm not ready for it to end.

I'm granted another few seconds of peaceful happiness before my eyes wrench themselves open with anger and disappointment, all directed back on myself.

How dare you fall asleep?

How could you leave Carter unprotected?

You are an exhausted, useless, shitty protector. You don't even deserve to look after him.

"NO! STOP IT! STOP!"

I sit up, aware of the early sunlight from outside. It's pushing through the curtains and duvets on the windows, in here and across the landing in Angela's bedroom. The soft light brings a sense of life back to the house, an unseen power, and defeats the darkness with ease.

It is almost silent now, except for some gentle breaths from Carter. He is fidgeting in his sleep, content on the pillows next to me. I do hope his dreams, if he had any, were peaceful and brought him joy.

Get up. Start moving. Make it real. Turn that dream into a reality. It is now a premonition, a glimpse of the future that awaits you ... but only when you get up. Make your way home and sit with them both at the kitchen table.

Chapter twenty-one

I have an idea where I want to be by this afternoon, yet I'm also forcing myself to be realistic as well, I have no choice. If I was travelling on my own, I could make it all the way home in just over a couple of hours.

I look at the map on my mobile's screen and ignore the fact that I haven't had a phone call, or a single attempt at contact, from anybody.

I can't accept it. I don't want to.

My thoughts linger with the hurtful truth, stinging my eyes with newly forming tears. I don't want to believe that everyone has disappeared … or changed. For now, as a second skin of hope, I'll cling to the other theories. Broken mobile phone towers are preventing any calls or messages getting through, people were taken to safe areas by the police and military, and thousands of scientists are working on the problem. An end to this nightmare world *is* in sight. I'll still take the coma with welcoming arms as well. Any different reality where this isn't happening.

I … can't accept it, I think, momentarily faltering with my belief, pushing the words along. They are heavy and weigh down on my mind, like the beginnings of a crushing headache.

••

It is nearly half past eight, and I have over seven hours of daylight to move in, however, there will be stops along the way. Carter will need to be changed and have his formula milk, I'll need to eat and rest as well, plus, and I sincerely hope it isn't the case, we might need to hide if we encounter someone. The woman across the road yesterday was the strictest teacher that I have ever studied with. I will never forget the important lessons she taught me.

Everything is done here. It's time. Oh, wait. Painkillers for your wrist. Take a couple now.

Carter is clean and dressed in his pushchair, recently fed, and I have bags of supplies with me, probably too many. I'm exhausted, I look overwhelmed, but I am ready. My mind is trying to turn my actions to positives, trying with all its might to feed my encouragement.

"Shall we go?" I ask Carter.

His glorious face beams at me from inside the thick, blue body suit I put on him earlier. One of his hands unintentionally waves at me, although it is covered in a mitten. He stares at it with curious eyes, probably wondering where his little fingers have disappeared to.

I moved the piano back to the lounge earlier this morning, so, with a cleansing breath, I open the front door and look outside.

Is that … Angela's gate? I ask myself, seeing the twisted piece of metal in the middle of the road.

Calm down!

I shut the door immediately and try to ignore the thumping heartbeat flooding through my ears.

I can't! I can't! I CAN'T! It's so close, too close! We were only upstairs! I didn't hear anything!

I want to call myself many derogatory names as I step back. I push my legs forward with a defiant strength, unwilling to let this fearful moment win.

Open the door.

I open the door again and scan the street, checking

every shadow, every doorway, and every corner in sight. I need to see and feel the presence of safety, even though it will be something that is almost impossible to achieve.

I grab the pushchair and wheel it out to the path. My right hand touches the meat cleaver for courage as the cold air hits my face.

"Train station, up the hill to the high street, head towards home. Okay, Carter?"

"Hnnna," he replies.

"Yes, we can do it. I totally agree."

'Remember, Shayla, steady pace, and listen to your body. If it tells you to stop and rest …'

"I'll stop and rest," I whisper, distracted by the advice inside my head.

The random voice belongs to my friend, Lauren, and I don't understand it straight away. It takes me a few seconds to realise why I have remembered her at this moment.

A lot of people have been through a 'get fit' stage in their lives before. Some start to visit a gym, or buy training equipment for their home. They promise themselves that it *will* get used, they *will* keep going, they *will* add a workout into their day. Many keep this promise, many do not. I would not like to guess how many gym membership cards go unused in a year, or how many sets of weights are in a corner right now, gathering dust.

I jogged for three months. I know, it's impressive, right? I surprised myself with the longevity of my commitment, and the amount of enjoyment it gave me as well.

I used to run along the seafront a couple of times a week. I'd head from my house to Leigh-on-Sea, a distance of about three miles, then back again. Of course, returning home afterwards was a glorious feeling. I had my bed, kitchen, cold drinks, shower, comfortable sofa, the foot spa Mum bought me for one of my birthdays … I could continue with all the home comforts, but I think you understand. I exercised, I pampered myself as a reward. The system works, well, mine did.

Seven miles to my house. Seven miles is not far.
Seven miles is NOT far.

About halfway along one of my seafront runs, I stopped for a drink of water and a minute or two of stretching out my legs. That is when I first met Lauren. She was doing the same, and looking much healthier and knowledgable than I ever could. We started talking and ended up finishing the rest of the route together. Over the next few weeks we trained at the same times, and she immediately became the pace setter, she pushed me to keep going. I mean, she was planning to run a marathon, so I couldn't help but be impressed with her strength, mental and physical, plus her positive attitude.

Our exercise based friendship lasted for just over a month, then, sadly, she changed her route to a more testing distance. We keep in touch with each other on social media, and through the occasional text message or phone call.

Thanks, Lauren. I hope you ran away from all this. I hope you ran as fast as you could and found a safe place to hide.

I start moving along the path at a brisk speed, fearful with every step. The slightest change in my surroundings causes me to panic. It is usually just a tree branch moving, or the sun's reflection in a window, but I keep expecting to see *her* as well, hidden in another doorway. The eyes will be closed tight and her body so still.

This is ... it's ...

I'm lost for words again. I ran out of the door at Amy's and saw destruction and death. I've been surrounded by the same scene for a couple of days now, yet it still won't register in my mind properly. It cannot be real.

I don't usually watch war films, although I have seen a few. If one of my favourite actors or actresses is starring in it, I'll give it a go. I've also watched in shock when the news bombarded me with images and video from real war zones. This is comparable. This is like a battlefield, only the silence is out of place. There are no soldiers shouting here, no guns firing, no visible conflict.

I used to think I wouldn't be able to handle such situations. I am too cowardly, too afraid of violence or pain, and unable to intentionally cause harm to others. I still believe this all to be true, yet I *am* in it now. I *have* to handle it, afraid or not.

As I near the back of the train station, I see a line of immobile carriages. They are a few hundred feet down the track, as if they have just left the platform. A couple of them aren't straight on the tracks, as if they have been pushed off the rails.

Those must weigh so much! Are they really that strong? The anger can push over a train carriage?

The hairs on my neck spring up again, and my stomach tightens. I let the darker thoughts return. I let myself imagine that kind of strength attacking Carter and me with ease. My heart races and my legs slow down.

Should I just walk along the train tracks? I ask myself, glad of the distraction. *Have I already thought about that? I can't remember.*

The line is a direct route to the top of Southend High Street, but I wonder if Carter's pushchair would be able to make it along the uneven ground. If anything I'd be hindering my progress, adding time to the journey instead of making it shorter.

Make a bloody decision!

I feel like Rory Gilmore, scribbling out one of her pro-con lists.

As I walk closer and stare at the attacked train carriages, I see the smashed windows, dented metal panels, and blood stains on the ground. They are spattered in random patches that cover a wide area. I don't even want to imagine what happened here, although I'm eager to investigate. I can't believe I am actually considering it.

Stay on the roads! You can't take Carter down there ... you'll both be too exposed. Where will you hide when the sun goes down?

I agree and fully commit to the rushed choice, without even breaking my stride. I carry on with my steady march as I head up Crown Hill.

Slow down! Take it easy on this part. You'll be exhausted before you've even walked for half an hour.

It's not my voice, it belongs to Lauren again. I listen, obey, and most importantly, lower my pace. This is going to be a tiring day, I already know that. I'm exhausted because of the broken sleep I've endured over the past couple of days, plus the endless mental assault.

Don't give up ... don't. You have to keep going.

This journey home will be an extreme form of exercise, however, there won't be any pampering session when I reach the next house. No foot spa, no fresh clothes, no sneaky masturbation in the shower as the hot water runs all over my skin.

What? Why are you thinking about that?

I have no clue as to why orgasms have entered my head, especially when I am surrounded by this version of the world. I am full of adrenaline, though, I know that much. The constant danger is providing a powerful thrill. It is so misplaced and random, I have no choice but to smile and leave it in my thoughts.

Focus!

I tell myself the next house will belong to a foot spa saleswoman, *and* she has loads of them stacked in a room. Yeah, I'm that lucky, I am. I'll be spoilt for choice, able to pick from hundreds of different models, maybe even find a prototype for a foot rubbing, massaging, your-feet-are-going-to-love-this, deluxe 3000! It's made of solid gold, and the buttons are diamonds. No, wait, it's made of ... chocolate, yeah, chocolate, and the buttons are ... even more chocolate.

A steady stream of water runs down the hill next to me, heading towards the drains along the kerb, and the air is putrid. I have been trying to ignore it since we left Angela's, however, it is growing more potent.

I stop walking and open the large changing bag I have attached to the front of the pushchair.

"It's in here somewhere, I know it is. I'm sure I saw it this morning when I packed everything up!" I say, growing frustrated as I rummage through a handful of clean nappies, wipes, and bibs.

"Got it!" I say as I find a small pot. I think I've spoken too loudly and spin my head around in panic.

We're okay. We're okay, I think, almost believing myself. The shadows are alive in my mind, hiding the anger. *Where do they all go during the day? How many of them are out actually here?*

I hold the pot of menthol rub in my hand, unscrew the top, and hope my idea works. I know I've seen someone do this before in a movie, or on a television series.

I dab some of the ointment under my nose, touch the collar of my coat, then rub the rest on the front of Carter's body suit.

"There you go, little man. That should make it less stinky for you!" I say, adding a silly voice. I very much doubt the stern face, the one I've been wearing since we left Angela's, has been enjoyable for Carter to look at all the time.

I take a deep breath and smile with a mild sense of accomplishment. The menthol scent is masking every other odour. It is strange how the small triumphs help me so much, however, I do understand why.

After another minute or so, the top of the shops along Rayleigh High Street come into view. I'm bewildered to see early decorations on display, in preparation for the Christmas season.

Christmas. I'd actually forgotten about it. It's only about four weeks away. How could I have forgotten? How?

I stop moving as future plans, some already held for so many years they are practically a tradition, flood back through my head.

I would be going shopping with Mum soon, for decorations.

113

We'd bring them home and add a red and gold theme, beautifully lit, to the entire house. I'd ask her leading questions about what she wanted, then buy her as many gifts as I could afford, and she would do the same to me. Drinks with my friends ... nights out clubbing ... mountains of food ... opening the presents ... Joan from next door popping over for a few minutes, only for it to turn into hours and seven more cups of tea. Tammie's kids knocking on the door with cards and paintings they'd made for me and Mum ... the excited looks on their faces when I grab their chocolates and money. Shit! How could I have ... have forgotten?

I realise I have stopped moving. It's as if an invisible wall has been built in front of me, keeping me in place, forcing me to deal with the changed world.

"Carter, I'll get you some tinsel for your pushchair, I promise."

I wanted a smile, or any reaction to be honest, and he delivers with a beautiful grin and a gentle squeal. I knew he would save me.

I notice a strange noise, one growing louder, as I near the top of Crown Hill. It's the sound of steadily running water.

Where's that coming fr ... oh, it's a burst water pipe.

I see it in front of me, in the middle of the road, yet I have to stare for a few seconds before all the details add together, *and* make sense.

The reason I had a moment of confusion is because pipes are always placed under the ground. This one has been ripped up through the concrete and tarmac. I can see a line of raised road, bordered by large chunks of concrete and dirt, where the pipe has been pulled.

Once again, the pure and ... inhuman ... strength on display sends pulses of fear through me.

But ... the woman across the street from Angela ... she was human ... she wasn't ... a monster ...

I look left and right, and start to absorb the damage to the high street itself, as well as the shops along it. My eyes are trying to process the scene, however, with every second

114

that passes, I notice something new. It is exactly the same as when this began, when I left Amy's and saw the car in the middle of the road for the first time. The story unravelled in front of my eyes, with new details becoming apparent with every millisecond that ticked along.

Here and now, I see evidence of burnt out fires, random destruction to shop fronts, Christmas decorations and tinsel covered trees scattered across the streets and road, the water pipe that hypnotised me a moment ago, and broken glass.

So much broken glass.

Their are mounds of it dotted about, like huge stacks of diamonds, and the sun this morning is hitting every shard, causing beautiful and multicoloured rays to spin before my eyes.

To my right there is an overturned bus, surrounded by a shallow and wide layer of water. The roof is facing me at an angle, glistening in the sun because of the spray and ripples from the pipe.

What was that? Oh, it's just … another reflection …

More movement follows near the back of the bus, like an out of place shadow. I've seen too many of those this morning.

Is it? Is it a reflec … SHIT!

I step back too quickly, panicked and caught off guard, and trip on a piece of wood that must have been snapped off a nearby bench.

My first thought is of Carter. He doesn't seem phased, fortunately, and remains silent in the pushchair.

Get up! Get up! GETUPGETUPGETUP!

I stand and focus my eyes on the bus again, hoping I've made a mistake, hoping my thoughts about the reflections were correct.

No, something is moving … someone. Are they … under the bus? I can see their hand and arm!

It flaps and claws at the road, like a possessed limb

115

living on after the body has long died. I'm sure I've seen a movie in the past with a similar scene in it, probably starring my scared teenage actress.

Run! Run! RUN!

I turn my head left and right, hurting my neck in the process with such swift movements. I need to choose an escape path and get away from here.

No! Wait! Wait a second ... think.

My mind races as thought after thought pounds loudly. They're all shouting at me to listen, to take my unexpected chance to learn.

'It's not ideal, Shayla,' begins Charlie's voice, 'but it *is* a great opportunity for study. When else will you find one of them trapped like this, if at all?'

"Are you fucking serious?" I ask through gritted teeth, directing my question at my own thoughts. "You want me to get ... closer?"

No way! No fucking way! I can't. I need to keep Carter away from here.

The cleaver is firmly in my hand, although I have no memory of actually grabbing it.

'The subject appears to be contained. You do have a high probability for success,' says Charlie. I have no choice but to laugh, losing myself in the surreal moment. She uses that exact same line when we are out together and a fit guy is in sight.

'You are heading in that direction, correct? So, use the opportunity, Shayla! Photographs, video, your own interactions and opinions. It all counts. Learn everything you can.'

Charlie's voice is so clear, I wouldn't be shocked at all if she appeared next to me in the street.

This is ... madness! Have I lost my mind because I'm even considering it?

A very refined voice arrives in my head, belonging to an unknown male. He starts to talk about excepting fear, or

116

falling into the abyss of insanity. I suppose he is referring to the pool of congealed blood that keeps calling to me. Well, that's how I interpret his words.

You've spoken to me before. You're the main character in that book! I think, recognising his tone.

His words are an eloquent mixture of my own memories from the book, my new fears, and my ignored longing to dive towards the blood.

It will be so peaceful there ...

The turning into Eastwood Road is in view, a few hundred feet ahead of me, and I could make it there quickly with a sprint, even with the pushchair.

It's a stupid idea ... utterly stupid ... however, I thought the same about the mobile phone last night, and that worked. We are going that way ... but ... if this goes wrong ... if it attacks us ... where could we run to?

I find every doorway and the alleys between buildings as well, imagining the worst. I picture it in my mind, allowing my darker fears to play out. I have to know that If I walk around the bus, and *it* gets loose, we'll be able to escape.

I stand there in a strange sort of trance, surrounded by the pumping water, debris from all the shops, and vandalised vehicles. I grab my phone, subconsciously, and strengthen my grip on the cleaver as well. I arrange and rearrange them on the pushchair and in my hands. I have to move Carter with complete control, have my weapon close, *and* record video.

I'll put the cleaver on top of the bag, so I can grab it easily. I'll record the video as I push with the other hand. Right?

I agree with myself a few seconds later, although I don't move an inch. Hesitant thoughts, powerful and ever present, are pushing down on my body, once again grounding me like a statue.

I take a deep breath and walk forward, slowly. I move to the buildings, as close as I can get, and point my phone at the bus.

Step by step. We'll be okay ... we will be okay!

I steer the pushchair through some glass and bricks, then, with a sharp inhale, stop moving.

It's another woman!

I almost drop my phone because my hand is shaking so much. "Oh ... fuck it!" I whisper. Such was my fear, I forgot to even start the recording.

I steady myself, click the screen, and move a few more steps. I flick a glance at Carter and make sure that his dummy is in.

She's ... I ... where ... I'm unable to create a coherent line of thought and need to take a breath. *Where are her legs?*

I want to turn away, run, scream in disgust. Instead, I simply stare, unable to take my eyes off of her.

Her eyes are closed, exactly like the other woman's were. I was right, they do look like healed scars. What does that even mean? Can she still open them? Can she even see me? Why would this happen to people?

It is impossible to even guess at an age, her face is too dirty with wet streaks from the water, what seems to be blood, and old make-up. She has black hair, straight and stuck across her face in strands, plus a bruise on her neck. I think there's a cut there as well, or a similar injury.

What happened to you?

As I try to answer myself with random scenarios, I decide she is also young, just as the woman across the street was. Her top is short-sleeved and I think I can see a sequinned heart pattern on the front, despite the angle and amount of dirty water.

My body and my mind, even my soul as well, are all prisoners in the strangest, most vivid moment of my entire life. I don't want to study her any longer. I don't want to see more of the horrific injuries she has sustained, yet I cannot move. I *need* to stay here, to have my eyes fixed on this near dead human. Every contradiction battles out in my imagination, each negative equally as powerful as the positive. I want to talk to her but stay silent. I want to touch her skin but keep my distance. I want her to die but wish I could rescue her.

Did the bus fall on top of her? Did the anger push it over without any care for her? They don't care about injuring one of their own?

Fortunately, because of the position of the bus, I can't see much of her lower body. I can see the blood around her, though, rippling with the water, and it reminds me too much of the dark pool.

She hasn't noticed us yet, has she?

Yesterday, my mannequin enemy stood for so many hours. This woman, she is gently clawing at the floor, and lifting her head up and out of the water every few seconds.

I tap the screen on my mobile phone, put it away in my pocket, and start to move away. My stomach tightens and threatens to make me vomit.

Okay, move! We've done enough!

I manage about two feet before the wheels of the pushchair run over a piece of glass, about the size of an A4 sheet of paper. It smashes and the sound dances through the air on the icy breeze.

The woman opens her mouth widely, as if she is about to scream, growl, or roar. Nothing happens, though. She can't physically produce any other sounds apart from forced and grating breaths.

What the fuck?

Despite her fatal injuries caused by the bus toppling over, ones that will take her life very soon, the woman begins to punch and thump at the road underneath her body. She claws with disregard for pain at the hard tarmac, trying to pull herself along, trying to get closer to me.

Not you! It's the sound of the glass. She wants to stop the sound!

Her eyes remain closed, yet she is facing me directly, somehow able to pinpoint the location of the noise. Her mouth opens to roar again, even though she can't, then snaps shut in frustration.

Please ... we have to go ... you must find the strength to move ... please.

The water by her waist swishes and ripples as she pulls her body forward, ignoring the excruciating pain it must be causing.

I push Carter through the broken glass and bricks, trying to find a smooth piece of path or street. I need to move fast instead of battling with the rough terrain.

'It worked, Shayla. You have collected some important information,' says Charlie's voice. 'I am wondering now, though, about the water.'

The water?

'Remember what we spoke about before? It had to start somewhere. Is it still spreading, and if so, how? Is that woman's blood carrying a pathogen, one that is now in the water?'

I reach Eastwood Road and am relieved to see it is a lot clearer than Rayleigh High Street. I can power my legs and the pushchair down here for a couple of minutes, until I see a suitable house with an open door. I need to sit down for a while and recover from what I just put us through, although Carter is perfectly content and unfazed.

'Shayla, when did you last drink any water?' adds Charlie.

Chapter twenty-two

I keep moving at a decent pace, still reeling from the sight of the woman.

Why did you do that?! Why? Stupid … fucking stupid!

Her actions have … changed me. They are subtle, yet I know they've happened. I see her torn apart and shredded body, the blood seeping from her injuries, and the furious expression on her face. They will all live inside my memory, forever.

I am surprised, though, by my ability to withstand being so close to her. I don't know where the courage came from, and I doubt any answers I do find will ever suffice. I cannot yet accept that level of self-belief, even though I'm witnessing it personally, living it every second. I still see myself as a coward, so it will be unwarranted and my mind will reject it.

My legs push me forward as I pass, yet also ignore, many of the houses. I could get inside any of them, I suppose, there isn't anyone around to stop me. I want more distance, though, and I must have it. I want to be miles away from that … thing.

Over there! Daws Heath Road … get inside one of them. Get inside and stop running.

I turn down the road and am able to keep jogging, even with the pushchair and all the bags. Carter laughs at me, so he seems to be enjoying the exciting, adventurous, and slightly turbulent pace.

I love your innocence, little man. I envy it. I wish I could see the world through your eyes.

The damage here is minimal, especially when compared to many of the other places I have seen since leaving Amy's. Seeing this eases a lot of the concerns I hold close about the anger.

I wonder for a few seconds about their behaviour. If they follow a pattern, *if,* then we might be safer here, as opposed to a more densely populated area.

Right, enough. Find a place to rest.

I'm not being selective right now, I just want to be inside. To be honest, I don't trust myself to be selective. I'm not in the correct frame of mind to make concise decisions. A mistake now, even a small one, could mean … *No, don't think the word … don't! … could mean death … for … for both of us.*

I know I'll eventually watch the recording I took by the overturned bus, I *want* to, however, a part of me will fight hard against it.

Why would I want to relive that? Why would I want to see any of that, ever again? I … I wonder if she's dead yet?

I see an open door on the side of a house and head directly for it. I linger on my last question. I linger on the thought of death. It isn't like me to think about something like that.

I know I'm panicking as I near the door, it's growing more severe. I'm feeling sick and too confused as well, so I want a chance to take a breath and calm myself. It's all I seem to do at the moment. I live in an unending cycle of panic and recovery.

I move the pushchair through the door, straight into the house's kitchen.

"I'll be right back, Carter. Stay quiet for me, please," I whisper, making sure his dummy is in fully.

I grab the cleaver, close the front door as gently as I can, then walk through to the next room. I don't intend to inspect every inch of this house, I know I'm not staying here.

This must be the lounge, but it's a bit empty. There is only what's needed, nothing else.

The minimalist décor includes a sofa, long sideboard, large screen television, lots of different gaming equipment, a computer, and several black and white photographs on the maroon painted walls. They are of a few famous landmarks, yet I can't tell if they are his work or just generic prints.

Oh, wait a minute, I think this is a man-cave. Yeah, the den of a single guy, one very much enjoying being that way. I've had to create a few well timed excuses in the past so I could get out of places like this.

Despite the stories I've already told about my past history with boyfriends, I know when a guy is only after getting my underwear off. I've never been duped yet, so I must be doing something right.

The first face that appears inside my head is that of Joseph.

'Not Joe, only Joseph. Okay? Not Joe.'

He never told me why that was such a specific request.

Joseph … I'll give you credit where it's due, I thought about it. I really thought about it.

I met Joseph at *Delicia,* a modern bar near where I used to work. Many of us from the office went there, a bit too frequently, either during lunch or straight after our shifts finished. He worked in the same building, but for a different company. The funny thing is, if you were to ask me what he did there, I couldn't tell you. I know it had something to do with buying and selling land rights, nationally. Whatever his career choice was, it made him a lot of money, hence his own cave of manliness. Actually, I should stop with the masculine labels, because they are unfair assumptions. I'm not a feminist, as such, and I think the constant questions regarding men versus women are a tired and overused battle. It should have been retired a long time ago, so a more positive route could have been chosen. Does that make sense? It is more of

123

an issue because media bombardment keeps dragging it back up as one. In my opinion, it's time to move forward, so let's start moving, *together*.

While at the bar one evening, a few people arranged to go to one of the casinos in town afterwards. I expect it was just after pay day, so I had money in the bank, *and* the brandy made me feel like I couldn't lose. Those roulette tables were going to be my bitches. I'd own them. You get the idea.

I'd known Joseph for about six weeks by then, and had chatted to him for quite a few hours in the bar. Admittedly, some of those were blurred with alcohol, or interrupted by my dreadful attempts to sing along with the jukebox selection. We got on well, made each other laugh, and shared a mutual interest in thriller movies. Anything with a great twist at the end, or the opportunity to work out 'whodunnit'.

I do not go home with strangers, not ever, and I'm very proud of that. I've been tempted, of course, but I've never acted on that dangerous impulse.

Joseph wanted to go back to his flat and change first, so he invited me along with him. We would then be able to share the taxi fare, and I could check out his DVDs while I waited. That's how he sold the idea to me.

I wonder how many times that actually worked, Joseph?

On the way, as a safety precaution, I prepared myself. Many people out there, not just women, have done exactly the same before. I pretended to text friends while I actually created alarms on my phone, set to go off at various times in the upcoming hour. If I needed an escape, a reason to disappear, the alarms then become feigned phone calls from a friend in need. If everything is fine, I ignore them as emails, or calender notifications. Great idea, right?

That particular night, Joseph behaved himself, although he did decide to take a shower before we headed off to the casino. He walked about without a top on afterwards, apparently searching for a shirt, so I had no choice but to see his muscular torso.

Almost, Joseph, almost. You're hot and I was tempted, there's no doubt about it. That night, though, I was more interested in the casino, and I won over four hundred pounds on roulette.

I think of Amy's as I stare at the clock on the kitchen wall, and how it seems like weeks ago that I was there, not days. It's just after nine thirty, so we're making good time on our journey home.

As I find the stairs and head up, cautiously, I hear Carter in the kitchen, fidgeting in the pushchair.

"Boowaaa," he says.

"Yeah, boowaaa," I whisper back. "I'll be careful, don't worry."

Bathroom, small bedroom, and is that a home office? I wonder what this guy's job is? I think as I pass a couple of the open upstairs doors.

There are more photographs up here. I recognise Paris, London, and I think one of them is the Brandenburg Gate in Berlin. If he did take all these, he loves to travel, and is also very talented with a camera. The black and white of the prints seems to always bring out a sense of loneliness, though. It could be intentional, as in that is his theme or style when taking photographs. I kind of hope it is in a way. I will never meet the man, yet I would still feel for him if he had those thoughts, and the emotions that breed from them.

The bedroom. I bet this place has a few stories to tell me.

Mum used to say things like that, and other similar lines, especially over a cup of tea with Joan. They used to talk about their respective love lives, and it usually turned a little kinky, and sometimes quite erotic, after a while.

'Ooh, I saw a fit bloke working in the supermarket the other day. I asked him to get me something off of the top shelf, just so I could see his jeans wrap around his arse!'

I smile at the memories as I look about, once again, at very little furniture.

I like it, the style here in this house, but it feels so empty. To each his own, I suppose.

There is a bed with an ornate metal frame, and I love the design. It's dark-grey, as is the carpet, blinds on the window, and the painted border that runs horizontally around the room. It's very angular and crisp, organised. The walls are a medium-beige, matching with the pine wardrobes, dresser, and bedside tables. It works for me, I do like neat and tidy lines.

I search around a little, yet find nothing of interest … until I reach the dresser.

Oh my days! I think as a huge grin spreads across my face.

In the bottom drawer, I find a few cock-rings, some 'tantalising' gel, handcuffs, a bullet vibrator, and a selection of porn DVDs.

I laugh. I laugh some more as I take the bullet and one of the DVDs.

As was the case with Angela's house, there is no damage inside. I don't care about the garden, I just want us both to be safe and warm indoors for a short amount of time.

Maybe watch the porn? Wait, no! Stop it! Why do you keep thinking about sex?

I return downstairs to Carter, and put my 'borrowed' items in one of the bags. I also wrap the meat cleaver up in its towel covering, and put it on the kitchen worktop, easily in reach and view.

Carter suddenly rubs at his face and lets out a sharp cry. I can see a scratch on his right cheek.

"Oh, baby boy! What have you done?"

I take him out of the pushchair, give him a soothing cuddle, and gently kiss his injured face.

"I guess we can stay here for a little while, right? It isn't going to slow us down too much if we rest for half an hour. When is your bottle due, eh?"

I carry Carter through to the lounge and change his nappy. He rubs at his sore cheek and also pulls at his ear.

This might be because of what he has just done, for no reason at all, or because it's a sign of early teething.

Did I bring the gum gel with me from Susan's? I'll put some antiseptic cream on his face as well.

I search through the bag I have set aside for only Carter's supplies. Fortunately, I find what I am looking for almost straight away.

"This'll help, little man. You'll feel much better," I say in a very gentle voice. I hope it doesn't sting too much.

I spread gum gel thinly across the end of his dummy and hope my preventative measures help him. On a selfish note as well, I hope it will keep him silent in the hours and nights ahead. He needs to be quiet and not attract the attention of the anger, and I will do as much as I possibly can to make sure he stays that way.

I rub a little dab of antiseptic cream on his ridiculously soft skin, then grab his bottle. It might be a bit early to sit down and feed him, but there's no harm in offering.

"Hungry? Do you want some of this?"

Carter takes it with a smile and an excited wriggle, so it isn't that much earlier in his routine.

I'm trying, Carter. I want to keep some normality for you, even though there isn't really any left in this world.

I shuffle slightly on the cream sofa, so I can grab my mobile phone out of my coat pocket. It's difficult because I have to hold the bottle awkwardly. Carter grumbles at me because I have disrupted his comfort.

I should watch it, shouldn't I?

Indecision, one of my constant companions over the last few days, returns. I hold my mobile phone and my thumb hovers again.

'Remember what I asked you about, Shayla?'

What? I ask inside my thoughts, snapping the word.

'When you were by the bus?'

My thumb moves away as I tighten my muscles and

take a deep breath, trying to ignore Charlie's questions.

I am not like her! I am not!

Carter jumps slightly. I must have tensed up my body too quickly and scared him without realising.

"Sorry, I'm so sorry. This is difficult, Carter. I can't bring myself to think about it, do you understand?"

Carter reaches up and strokes my face, as if a slight breeze has danced around me. It is the most gentle, needed, perfectly timed response I could ever have received as a reply.

I cry a few tears. I take it to mean that he doesn't believe it either. He knows I haven't changed, and his soft touch was used to convey that to me without words. Perhaps he can sense it? Many people believe that babies are intuitive to emotions, and they can sometimes feel, or even see, things that others cannot.

"I am ... different, though," I say. "I can't explain it. It's inside ... under my skin ... *another me*."

Carter doesn't react this time. I think he is deliberately ignoring me now. I'm sure if he could roll his eyes at me, he would. And sigh. And moan. And roll his eyes again.

When did I last drink any water? Tap water, not bottled?

'Oh, finally!' says Charlie in a loud voice. 'Have you decided to think about it?'

Amy's? Angela's? I did have water at Amy's, I know I did. I was worried about the noise of the tap attracting the anger. I'm sure of it!

I lift Carter up and rub on his back as I think, rethink, and think again until I can feel a headache starting. I need to piece my memories back together.

I've only had bottled drinks since then. No tea. No water.

'That's great to hear. You were at Amy's on Tuesday, so I'd have expected symptoms to present themselves by now, judging by the evidence.'

Evidence?

'Your time spent ill was a timeline. It is a base to work from, yes? This anger, this change in behaviour, it began on

Friday evening.'

I do understand, I do, but what about everything else? The pool of blood? Did they see it? I never dreamt of anything like that before all of this. What about the hatred I felt towards the woman across the road from Angela's? All the violent thoughts I've had as well, even the ones in which I get hurt, or Carter does …

A tear falls down my cheek.

And you as well, Charlie. All the voices that speak to me. I shouldn't be able to hear any of you.

There is no answer. I know why, it is obvious, yet I don't want to accept it.

If I do change, if I do turn into one of them … the anger … will I …

My eyes land on Carter and his radiant smile.

… hurt him?

I cry more, this time through genuine sorrow. The thought of it upsets me so much and makes me feel ill.

I suddenly think of Susan's house, particularly the kitchen door when I arrived there. The glass was on the outside, I remember noticing it at the time.

Is this why Susan smashed her way out of her own house? She made Carter safe, then ran away and left him? She knew the anger was spreading inside of her, and felt herself changing?

I wish I could give myself some answers.

"Susan … she deserted her own son … to keep him alive?" I murmur under my breath.

I wonder if I will ever have to do the same as I realise that Carter has his eyes stuck on me, as if he is picking my thoughts apart. I stare at his face and scream in my mind. *NO! It will not happen! It will never, ever, fucking happen!*

I do believe myself, I do, although I have many tears on my face. I imagine Susan lived through this exact situation as well. Did everyone else out there promise themselves the same? Was there a moment for all of them, a crisis of morality, of constraint, of self-belief?

"I'm not ill, Carter. I am not!"

129

Carter chews on his fingers and smiles at me. "Voounn!"

"Yeah, let's go."

I look at my mobile phone. I click through to the video I recorded, the video I put myself through too much fear and stress to obtain.

I don't need it ... I don't ...

Without a second more of thought, I click the bin icon and delete it.

'Oh, okay. I didn't expect that,' says Charlie's voice, surprised by my decision.

Chapter twenty-three

The next hour and a half of the journey was a long stretch of road, however, we only managed to cover about two miles.

This is tough! Keep going … stay positive … don't give up, don't you dare give up!

I listen to my aggressive thoughts, although it is difficult for me to keep any sense of motivation. I am mentally and physically drained, freezing cold because of the chilled breeze, and scared. I can't pull my mind away from all the fear, despite how hard I am trying. I know I have Carter with me, but being out here, cloaked every second by the desperate solitude, it is unforgiving. With every step I see more evidence of the anger and their extreme power, their inexplicable rage.

It should have taken me less time to travel that short distance, about forty-five minutes or so. The street was covered in obstacles, though, the remains of past destruction. Wrecked cars again, uprooted trees, burnt out houses and shops, and even furniture that must have been thrown out of now deserted homes.

About half a mile along, I had to walk back on myself for a couple of minutes through some gardens. The street had been completely blocked, and I think it was intentional, like the cars I saw that were parked across front doors. I tried to picture it in my mind, to imagine the story behind their desperate actions. People must have known that *something* was coming, so they worked together to try and keep it at bay. All in one moment, the barrier managed to fill me with awe, sadness, hope, and more fear.

They must have been terrified. I wonder if they knew what was out here, or was it all just mass confusion, like with Samuel and Susan?

The 'wall' was created with at least twenty vehicles, all parked in lines, plus rubbish bins, pieces of wood, and I even saw a couple of wardrobes thrown on top of the cars. I fought back tears when I noticed that a child had placed a toy there as well. It was an action figure, some sort of medieval warrior. The plastic sword had been deliberately positioned, ready to attack.

They were panicking, that much is obvious. It was thrown together by everyone, made by impulse and terror.

Eastwood Road changes its name to Rayleigh Road halfway along, although I can't remember why, if I ever knew the reason at all. I'm further down that part of it now, at the bottom of Progress Road. It is lined with offices, warehouses, and factories. The top, where we are heading, leads to the back of Belfairs Woods. I see it as the edge of Leigh-on-Sea, and another step towards my goal.

We are a lot closer to reaching home. We are nearly there. Nearly there.

"I need to rest, Carter. Not for long, though, and eat as well. I'm starving," I say. "Oh, you're asleep. You're asleep … and I'm talking to myself. Great."

I take my mobile phone out of my coat pocket and check the time.

It's almost half past eleven. What shall I do now? I really want to get further along before I stop. I'm heading for Kelly's house, about another half an hour away.

Kelly, Amy's mum, lives on the other side of Belfairs Woods, and I've spent a lot of time at her home during my life.

So much time and so many memories, good and bad.

While growing up, I played there for hours, had

sleepovers, and sometimes raided Kelly's make-up, with her permission of course. I've eaten amazing breakfasts, lunches, and dinners, plus the barbecues in the garden as well. I can't even guess at how much alcohol I drank there over the years. Kelly made sure there was a bottle of brandy in the house, just for when I visited.

Be careful. These memories are amazing, but they'll ... they'll hurt you as well. Why do you think everything has started to make you feel different?

I close my eyes for a second, trying to ignore my warning, trying to hold on to the memories as they flood through me with a loving warmth.

I have to give credit to our parents, well, our mums. Kelly and Amy used to live near us before they moved to Leigh. It is sometimes all too easy to promise someone that you will keep in touch. Before you even realise it, weeks have passed by, maybe months, and life carried on around you.

I'm so glad that didn't happen.

Promise Mum and Kelly did, and they never broke it. They came to visit us, we went to them. Birthdays, over Christmas, New Years Eve ... for no reason other than to see each other.

'It's Sunday, so why not?'

'I've got a dentist appointment in an hour, can you keep an eye on Amy for me?'

'We're going to town for new shoes. Meet us for lunch, my treat!'

You're not ill. You feel different because you've started to believe the truth. You've known since the first day at Amy's, haven't you?

I consider screaming. If I do, I might drown out the thoughts.

They have all gone. Everyone you loved or cared for. Gone. You and Carter are the only people left.

"No," I whisper, "I'm not letting her go. I won't."

You need to accept it. She's gone. Mum has gone.

"No."

133

Chapter twenty-four

I stare up Progress Road for a couple of minutes, wrapped in its desolate and solemn presence. Two lanes, both of them empty of vehicles, flow down towards me. I see a grey, cold, concrete river, one stopped in time and stagnant.

My mind wrestles with the previous thoughts, the unbearable truth I do not want to confront.

"No. Don't say it!"

The silence all around me multiplies my sorrow, makes my thoughts even more hurtful than they already are, and claws at my heart without remorse.

Don't scream ... don't scream ...

I move back quite a few steps and turn away from the pushchair. My hands keep making fists, I can't keep my body still, and my lungs don't get enough air when I breathe.

Wha ... what is th ... this? A panic attack?

I force in a lungful of air, hold it, then bring my coat sleeve up to my face. I bury my mouth around the fabric and let the cry out. It needs to be set free, to swim through the emptiness.

The storm, your storm ... you worried about this at Susan's ... you knew it would happen ...

I stamp at the floor with as much strength as possible, trying to release all my rage and sorrow. It makes the soles of my feet sting and ache. I clench a fist and even hit my own hips and thighs. *Let it out! Scream until it's all fucking gone!*

"You aren't the only ones here ... you haven't won, not yet," I say, my mouth still on my coat. The words are quiet and gentle. I actually wanted them aggressive, yelled, and intense.

That's enough ... enough ...

My stomach tightens, cramps, then sends me forward with a punch of pain. I retch a couple of times, then vomit on the street. My throat pulls with terrible spasms as I wait for the unexpected sickness to end.

"Do you ... you hear me? You haven't won yet."

I splutter the words out as my body straightens back up. My face is the epitome of both fury and distress.

Carter stirs behind me with a gentle noise. He isn't moaning at all, so I don't worry too much.

One second, little man. Give me one second. I don't want you to see me in this state. I'm a mess.

I walk slowly back to the pushchair to find him stretching out his arms.

Water ...

I grab a bottle from one of the bags, take a swig inside my mouth, then spit it out on the street.

"Hey, baby boy," I say with a smile, even though it is forced, and grab the pushchair for some support. "I'm sorry if I woke you up. I needed to do that, to be really loud. Do you understand?"

Carter smiles at me, then he moans, then he grows a serious and questioning frown. The skin on his forehead creases up slightly and I feel as if a shrunken old man is about to chastise me for my erratic behaviour.

Of course he understands! He's just like you.

"Like me?" I whisper, speaking to my own thoughts.

Yes ... you ... you selfish bitch! Carter hasn't seen his mum for a couple of days. JUST LIKE YOU!

I accept the scathing words without question, then take Carter out of the pushchair and hold him close to me. "I'm sorry. I am," I say as I gently kiss his face.

135

I smile, slightly less emotional after my cry of inner pain. "I'm fine now. Look, I'm smiling," I say, lying completely.

Carter squeals with a smile, a kick of his legs, and a flap of his arms. I'm glad the frown swiftly disappeared, it wasn't his usual demeanour and I much prefer the adorable grins he wears for me.

Suddenly, as the silence wraps around my body, as the grey river calls for me to walk against its concrete and rigid current, my mind begins to purge itself of all thought. I feel light-headed and fear for Carter.

Don't fall! What's happening?!

I inhale, slowly, feeling the bitter air as it hits my lungs. I bend my legs, put one hand on the floor, then sit down on the road.

Calm, Shayla. Calm. It's because you fought back, because you let yourself believe. It's ... too much ... too much ...

I breathe out.

Fuck you, anger, fuck you! I can survive, I've got this far! FUCK YOU! This is my world ... MINE!

My fingers rub on the street. I want to feel the freezing and brittle concrete as it scratches at my skin. I need the harsh sensation to pull my mind back, *if* it can.

I'll take it, the pain. For you, Carter, I'll take it.

I am unsure if there has ever been a true epiphany before in my life. I mean, I've had a few eureka moments, a lightbulb-over-the-head, we all have. If someone asked me about a definite epiphany, though, I wouldn't have replied with a yes.

Until now.

My world ... our world ... survived ... still alive ... mine ... ours ... mine ... alive ...

The realisation that my life has now opened up for me, that I have been presented with an incredible freedom, sends strong pulses through my body. Charlie would love to study me as I sit here. She'd list all the neurochemical processes at work, plus the physiological and emotional changes they've set in motion.

You survived. Survived. You're a survivor. Survived. Still alive. Alive.

I am a different person again, now high on fear, excitement, possibilities, and risks.

I'm confined to the daylight hours, and I *must* accept that. It is the high price to pay, the rule I can never break. Everything I do in that time belongs to a new world, though, a new life.

All gone. Gone. Changed or dead. Dead. Survived. Alive. Not dead. Not dead.

I will have to live every upcoming second with the sorrow of losing those I love and care about. It will claw away at me and tear my mind and soul apart from the inside out. It will be extremely painful, mostly in an emotional sense. That is the balance. That is the negative to my new positive.

Except for Mum. I'm never letting you go. You are alive, somewhere. You are at home, hiding, safe. You taught me how to be the person I am toady. If I am still here, if I am still alive, you have to be. You have to be. You can't leave me, Mum … YOU CAN'T!

Carter leans forward. He grabs my face and starts to chew, kiss, and nudge with his mouth and lips.

Baby boy …

I immediately choke out a stifled cry. His affection is so powerful, it threatens to finally break me.

"Awww, you're such a little cutie! Are you giving me kisses? Are you trying to cheer me up? Are you?" I say through uneven gasps of air. Tears are falling over my lips, yet I have to smile. I have to.

Carter has laughed before a few times. This, though, is a full on burst of red-faced chuckling, one that only a baby can create.

Did I do that? Have I really made him that happy?

My mind purges itself again, however, every thought is replaced with amazing images that I do not recognise.

Your life together. This is what it could be like. Your unwritten story.

I see Carter smiling at me as I open my eyes in the morning. His first steps in the lounge at home. Playing with toys in the garden as the sun beams down at us both. Presents on birthdays and at Christmas. Sitting together in a warm and loving embrace, watching his eyes slowly close as he drifts off to sleep.

"I'll try to make it all happen. No, I *will* make it happen. For you."

Carter flaps his arms, bites on my cheek as a reply, and I feel something hard on my skin. My assumptions about him teething earlier this morning were correct.

"Show me, Carter. Open your mouth for me and smile. Gimme a big smile!" I say in a silly voice.

It's already happening. Our future together. This is a moment I will never forget.

"I'll put some more gel on for you, baby boy. It's going to be a while yet, but you do have a couple of hard lumps on your gums."

Carter stares at me with a strange look on his little face. I wonder if it's because I changed my tone of voice. He's wondering why the 'silly lady' has started to talk seriously with him.

"You're getting teethies! You're getting teethies! Woohoo!" I say with excitement, and add a tickle under his arms as well.

Our time together since my epiphany, since my soul wrenching scream, nothing short of magical for us both, is suddenly interrupted by the intense odour of rotten food. I hate … yes, I will use that word despite its power … how this nightmare constantly takes any essence of good away from me. My almost complete acceptance of the new world, my mind fighting back with strength, and Carter's amazing laugh, those special moments are tainted now.

Fuck you! Fuckyoufuckyoufuckyou!

"Fudge you! Fudge you!" I shout, again changing my words to a child-friendly version.

"Come on, I'll put you back in the pushchair. We can have lots more cuddles later. I promise."

Once he is strapped back in, I rub more menthol under my nose, on my coat, and on Carter's pushchair.

"Right, let's get away from here. There are a lot of cafés along this road, and I think they're causing this rotten smell. Stink, stink, stinky!"

I hold my nose, puff out my cheeks, and Carter rewards me with another burst of chuckled laugh. It is the most beautiful sound in the world to me at the moment.

As we finally begin walking up Progress Road, I'm unsure if my legs are prepared, or strong enough, for the ascent. It isn't very steep, but the simple truth of the matter is that I'm exhausted. It hits me in sporadic waves, has done all morning, but I've been able to persist so far.

You have to do it. Distract yourself somehow. Think of anything but the pains in your body.

I start to imagine future shopping trips in my mind. With the unknown ahead of me in the days and weeks to come, it's such a strange sensation. I can, potentially, own *anything.* No budget, no restraint, no limit.

I can get a huge television for the house … in every room … books, clothes, trainers … jewellery … I could just walk inside a bank and take all the money!

"There's a few toy shops on the way home, Carter. We probably won't reach them until tomorrow now, though. I'll grab you loads of new toys when we get there! All the toys! Doesn't that sound great?"

As we near the top of the road, there is a large car showroom on the left. Again, my new desires spark and scream loudly at me.

"What do you think, Carter? Is it time for some fun?" I ask. The sun breaks through a cloud overhead and covers us both in a burst of warmth.

I don't wait for an answer. I act entirely on impulse and rush through all the parked vehicles outside, admiring their expensive designs.

"Hey," I say as memories from my past fly through my mind. "Do you know what is just over there, by the edge of the park?"

Carter remains silent. His eyes seem to be studying mine, as if he's wondering why the silly lady is getting excited again.

"There's a skate ramp in there … a half pipe. Shall we go in? Shall we?" I say. My voice raises its pitch with growing anticipation.

Again, I do not wait. I rush along the service road in front of the car showroom, running parallel to the main dual carriageway, the Arterial Road.

Straight down there, all the way to Priory Park … Victoria Avenue … nearly home.

I walk in Oak Wood Park and head straight for the ramp. The metal panels are slightly damp due to the time of year, streaked with droplets of condensation. I don't care, though, and step on. I smile wide and my heart beats faster.

I start to move, very slowly at first, turning the pushchair around when I am slightly up the curve of the ramp.

"Woohoo! Are we skating? Are we?" I cry with delight. The cold air hits my face with a sharp sting, yet I ignore it and laugh.

I push faster, walk a bit higher, and scream with pure delight. Carter laughs and smiles so much as he joins me in the very unexpected, and somewhat ridiculous, enjoyment.

I haven't really thought about anything fun for a long time. In fact, I can't even remember the last time.

"Whoa!" I yell as my boot suddenly hits an icy patch.

I fall down, burst out laughing, and my hand grabs the pushchair handle to stop Carter from rolling away off of the ramp.

"Did you see that, baby boy? Oh my days! Did you? I fell over! I landed on my arse!"

More hysterical laughter follows as I lose myself in the world. It shouldn't be allowed because almost everything in my life is an opposite now, yet we have defied that rule. Carter and I have fought together and broken through the anger, the darkness, the cold fear that covers everything.

'Well done, Shayla,' says my mum's voice. 'You've made that little boy so happy.'

I sit, smile, and let a couple of tears fall. *Thank you.*

I slowly get to my feet, rub my wet hands on my coat, then search through the bags I packed this morning. I don't know why I want one, but I'm after Susan's cigarettes.

"There they are," I say. "Right, let's go and look at these cars, yeah? I wonder if we can find any of the keys?"

I light a cigarette as I trace the road with my eyes, daydreaming about taking a car all the way home.

Chapter twenty-five

When I first stepped inside Angela's house, I loved it, and her, for providing me with such a safe haven. This place, unfortunately, creates the opposite feelings. It's so exposed, and there is too much space here.

Tall glass windows line three sides of the building, plus, because of all the cars inside, there are wide areas everywhere.

I wouldn't feel safe here. The anger could get in so easily ... and I'd have nowhere to hide ... nowhere to protect Carter.

I set the pushchair by an emergency exit door and take Carter out. He grabs at my hair and face with excited hands.

"I know! Look at all these cars! Wow! I bet they go reeeaaallyy fast, yeah? Vroom! Vroooom!"

I hold him safe and tight as I spin gently around in a full circle.

Carter smiles and laughs at me. I really can't get enough of it. It is the sound of our entwined lives, the song for our possible future.

I walk towards one of the cars, a black estate."What about this one? Do you like it?"

"Eerrgha."

"No? Okay, what about the blue car over there?"

Carter doesn't reply. He's found something on the ceiling to stare at, probably one of the long fluorescent lights, even though they are all over thirty feet away. The structural beams are slightly curved and painted bright white, with thick metal wires attached to them. For some macabre reason, one that I can't explain, they make me think of oversized bones. I feel as if I am about to tour the dinosaur exhibit in a museum.

"Ooh, wait a second. I love that one!" I say. My voice echoes slightly and the sound puts me on edge.

You are safe. They're not here. Just the echo, that's all.

I look around the showroom for a few seconds and hold Carter tight in my arms.

I really don't like this place.

I walk to the side of a maroon SUV, admiring its sleek lines and exquisite paintwork. I am not a car enthusiast, let me tell you that now, but I think this is truly beautiful. I want it.

I saw one of these outside as well.

I turn around and look at all the workstations and offices, located mostly on the mezzanine floor. The desks carry an eerie sense with them, as if someone is going to return at any second to continue their work day. There's even a half drunk cup of coffee on the nearest one to me.

I bet the keys are all in here somewhere.

"Let's have a quick look around, Carter," I say as I take the mobile phone out of my pocket. "It's quarter past twelve now, so we have a little bit of time to rest up."

We walk upstairs, then straight back down again. Carter needs a nappy change, so I grab his bag, plus some water and a few snacks for myself.

"You couldn't have done that five minutes ago?" I ask him, joking. "My legs hurt, baby boy! I need to sit down and chill out for a while."

Carter smiles as we reach one of the offices. I do as well when my eyes see the kettle on a cabinet in the back corner. It's surrounded by little paper packets of sugar and a box of milk pots.

Tea bags! Oh my days! TEA! I can have a cup of fucking tea!

I can't quite believe, or understand, why the idea is making me so excited. I suppose it is a dose of normality, a treat when I thought none were ever possible again, or because a cup of tea always makes me feel better. Either way, it has put a smile on my face, so I'm not going to overthink the reasons too much.

I change Carter, and make him laugh as well by telling him that he has a 'very stinky butt!'

I leave him on the changing mat with his fluffy elephant toy as I head for the kettle. I have a couple of bottles of water in my hand because I want to clean it out first. I don't trust the water now, not after my imaginary conversation with Charlie this morning.

"Now, are you watching carefully? This is an important lesson to learn. How to make a cup of glorious tea!" I say. I check the date on the milk and see, with erupting relief, that it is still safe for me to drink.

Carter chews on his elephant toy and ignores my enthusiasm completely.

Chapter twenty-six

Nearly twenty minutes pass by before I *think* I am satisfied with the cleanliness of the kettle. No, I *am*. There's no room for maybe right now. I rinsed it out with some of the bottled water, and boiled it up a few times as well. My patience was tested, but I'm so glad it behaved.

Carter is still on his changing mat, content, and enjoying a rather loud discussion with his fluffy elephant.

I wonder what you two are talking about? So funny!

From the amount of times he has chewed on the big blue ears, I'd say Carter is definitely winning.

I stare at the kettle, tap my fingers impatiently on the office desk, and chant along in my head.

A watched pot never boils. But … I need a cup of tea! A watched pot never boils. Of course it boils … it has to boil. If you're waiting for for it to boil, because YOU REALLY NEED A CUP OF TEA, it will seem to take longer than usual. If I urgently needed a taxi, it would seem to take forever to pick me up as I watched out of the window. A waited for taxi never arrives. A watched pot never boils. I NEED A CUP OF TEA! Hang on, why does that sound so familiar?

Another minute passes by until I'm holding up my drink with a smile. "Here we are, Carter. This, little man, is a cup of tea! Tea! Da-da-da!"

Carter gives my excitement one second of attention, then continues to talk with the blue elephant.

I drink as fast as I can and send my mind back to a

safer time, before all of this happened to the world. It is so strange how the mundane actions of my life, such as making a simple hot drink, were taken for granted.

When was the last time I had a shower? Cooked a proper meal?

I can answer the questions, but I don't want to. They are all making me frustrated and angry.

Without any further thought, I swipe my hand at the filing tray on the desk. It hurtles across the room, hits the wall to my left, and sends a dull echo through the car showroom.

Carter takes a moment to stare at me, then the tray on the floor a few feet in front of him.

I rub at the bandage on my wrist as the muscles shoot a few jolts of pain through me, and try to calculate how long it's been since I took painkillers.

A couple of low growls suddenly decide to answer my violent outburst.

No …

Another follows as I move closer to Carter, crouching my body lower to the dark-blue carpet inside the office. If I stay down, I'll be out of view if there is anyone on the ground floor.

They're in here? They're in here … with us! Shit! No sound, Shayla! No fucking sound at all!

I force myself to stay still as I look down at Carter with begging eyes. His dummy is in and, thankfully, the conversation with the blue elephant has finished.

Charlie? Mum? Someone help me!

No voices answer me. No words of advice respond to my terrified plea. My whole body is shaking and out of my control, I feel sick, and there is thick sweat pouring down my face and back.

I'm so sorry, baby, I think, aware of how many times I have apologised to him. I worry that I'm not looking after him at all and keep putting his life in danger. *Once again, you are an exhausted, useless, shitty protector.*

146

"I'll get us out of here, I promise," I whisper, my face inches from his, yet I regret the words immediately.

My thoughts are too random and impossibly fast. I cannot keep up with them as they pour like a raging waterfall, crashing down around me with power and unbelievable noise. I replay everything that has happened to me over the past few days, as if I am watching myself in a movie, pleading for an answer to present itself.

Think! Fucking think! Come on!

I watch the scenes play out. They are mostly sped up when considered useless, or at a normal pace if I want to give them some more thought.

I revisit Amy's, Susan's, and Angela's. I let the past fears return as I recall the video from Samuel, I stand in front of the train station and stare at the blood stained concrete, and I pity the woman under the overturned bus.

Some scenes from my memory stick inside my mind, some are thrown away quickly. I don't dwell on that which will upset or anger me.

It's still light outside. The woman at Angela's never moved. I've heard the anger cry out in the day, but they haven't attacked in that time, not yet.

I remember the young female, caught and horrifically injured under the bus in Rayleigh High Street. She seems to be an exception to the rule. She heard the noise I made, and reacted to it as expected of the anger, yet was that only instinctive? Would she have attacked me?

Who cares? Grab Carter and run!

I stand up, slowly, and my fear is suddenly replaced by a burning rage, an all consuming urge to fight back, to stand my ground. "I care. I'm sick and tired of running. I fucking care!"

A deep snarl rises from somewhere on the ground floor, caused by my raised voice.

My heart beats fast, yet I have now regained all the control. "Carter, please stay quiet," I say in a monotone

147

voice. It's akin to 'Tidy your room', or 'Go to sleep'. An order. A command. I want the words listened to and obeyed, without question.

I pick him up and deliberately avoid eye contact. I want Carter to realise how serious I am, how focused.

Shayla, what are you doing?

I grab everything of Carter's from the floor, walk out of the office, and head back to the pushchair. My mind hasn't faltered, it is clinging to the new resolve, the new fury I have created. I feel it burning inside, like a coiled serpent ready to strike its enemy.

'I don't like this side of you, Shayla. It scares me, a lot. Do you hear me, darling?' says Mum's voice. She has a recognisable tone coating her words, one of concern and growing anguish.

It sounded as if the growls came from over there, but I can't be sure. There are too many echoes in this building, it's so confusing.

I reach the pushchair and strap Carter in safely, ensuring that the dummy is still in his mouth.

"Remember, please be quiet." I say the words with a strict edge, even though he won't understand. I'm hoping my body language will reinforce them as well.

I grab and light another cigarette, then pick up the meat cleaver. It doesn't scare me that I am holding it with violent intent, with a vengeful purpose. It *should* scare me, make me feel hesitant, sick, raise a thousand questions of morality. I want every emotion and sensation to coat me, though, to force me to understand this moment.

The door to my right, the fire exit, is slightly open. I can't remember if it was like that when I first arrived.

I bang on the door with the side of the cleaver and, as expected, receive my response from the anger.

This is too fucking dangerous! What are you doing? You don't know how many there are!

I take a long drag on my cigarette as I push gently with my foot. I see a short hallway and another two doors.

*One leads outside, probably the external fire door? The other …
is that where they are?*

I cannot describe how I feel at this moment. I've
never experienced anything like it before in my entire life. My
mind is running along with so many thoughts, yet focused at
the same time. It is as if I am walking through a thick cloud of
memories, *and* possible scenarios. With every step, the dense
mist around me parts to clear a path. My body is in
contradiction as well. My heart races, yet I feel at peace. My
stomach cramps up with fear, my legs feel weak, but I can
sense the power inside. My muscles beg to be used, to unleash
their strength.

I want to … hurt them …

I walk into the hallway and grip the cleaver. My mind
tries to push Carter's face at me, to stop me from continuing.
I see his smile, his beautiful eyes, and the innocence he wears
every second. I ignore it all and move forward a couple of
steps.

*I'm coming for you! How does it feel? How does it feel to be the
… the prey? You WILL NOT scare us today! FUCK YOU!*

I raise the cleaver above my head as my blood pumps
through my body with too much rage, so much desire for
revenge. I kick the wall and hear a scraping breath from
behind the inner door.

'Shayla,' says Charlie's voice. It is next to me, inside
my head, and all around me. 'We spoke about this earlier.
You aren't changing. You are nothing like them.'

"Maybe I am!" I say through gritted teeth.

'No, you're not. You're not,' adds Mum.

"Get out of my head!" I scream.

The roars from behind the door are swift and fuelled
by the passionate hatred I have grown to recognise so easily.

Then, I hear Carter laugh.

Baby boy …

Another beautiful squeal follows.

Baby … Carter. My protector. I hear you.

I lower the cleaver as I quickly step back. My lungs empty themselves of all the air inside, and it doesn't feel natural, or under my control. I choke, retch, and hold my hand over my mouth.

There's a cigarette between your fingers.

I take a long drag, choke forcefully once more, and stare at my trembling hand.

What was I doing? I think as I stare up the hallway, towards the gentle sound of Carter's laugh. *I … I was so ready … so ready to hurt them … I wanted to. I wanted to cause pain …*

As was the case at Amy's, during my first night with the anger, I lose all sense of time. I'm standing with my back up against the wall, then I'm sitting, then I'm staring at a stack of cardboard boxes near the fire exit.

I need to move. Move. Need to. How long? Have I been here long? Carter. Baby boy. Move. I need to.

In a blur of thought and movement, I rush along the hallway. I grab the pushchair and hurry out of the doors, yet remember hardly any of the actions.

Why did I do that? What happened to me?

I ignore the questions. I'm no longer worried about any kind of infection, as I was this morning. I know my own mind and I know it was deliberate. It had nothing to do with changing, or becoming like the anger, it was simply vengeance. It was regaining control, *and* proving that I could keep it.

I get across the dual carriageway as I frantically light another cigarette. Nothing about the past twenty minutes makes any sense to me. I wish I could forget it, wipe it from my memory so there is only a dark cloud in front of my eyes when it threatens to return. It won't happen. It is there now, permanent, vivid, and dangerously raw.

Get to Kelly's! It's just after the bottom of this road! Not far … not far …

Chapter twenty-seven

I feel more like myself just by walking along these familiar streets. My uncharacteristic and sadistic urges are disappearing, replaced with potent memories. Yes, they contain lost friends, ones I will probably never see again, yet their strength fights through the darkness.

Is this my life now? Will I live with a constant battle in my mind as the dark attempts to distinguish the light?

I'm near the end of The Fairway, a road that borders one of the edges of Belfairs Woods. The houses in this area are expensive, often of an old-fashioned design, and they make me add something new to my 'shopping list'. *You can live anywhere now. Anywhere! As long as they are secure, or can be made that way* ... I take a pause as the scope of my imagination multiplies beyond its own limit. ... *Every house belongs to us now, Carter.*

Kelly only lives a few more roads away, about five minutes on foot at my current pace.

"I used to spend a lot of time around here, Carter. I had lots of fun when I was younger, playing in the woods, going on horse rides, and there are a couple of parks not far from here. I doubt we'll be able to visit them, though, not today."

As I reach a set of traffic lights, I stop and look at the shops on both sides of the street. There are only about ten, plus a pub, and a petrol station a few hundred yards further to my left.

"When you're older, I'll tell you lots of stories about the pub. Not all of them, though, only the … child-friendly ones."

Yeah, like that night you and Hayden ran to the petrol station to buy a box of condoms!

I smile as the memories return. Sex outside as the summer heat lingered, in the car park, was an exhilarating thrill.

I grow slightly annoyed at myself as I look at the various shops here. It should have crossed my mind earlier that I needed to restock my supplies, and Carter's as well. He is the most important part of my life right now. If I ran out of food or drink, I'd be hungry, thirsty, and pissed off with myself. I could handle that. He could not.

I'll need water, that's a must. Grabbing some medicines from the chemist will be extremely helpful in the future as well. Antibiotics, headache tablets, refills of all the gels and ointments in Carter's bag.

The list grows impossibly long in my mind. I'm glad to be near Kelly's house, almost safe, and that I'll be able to check through all the bags again soon.

You need to learn to trust yourself again. Trust your decisions, or you'll always be questioning them.

It's a profound line of thought, and I can't think of a better time for it to have arrived. I understand it, and listen to it. I know I have been lost over the past few days, my mind an uncontrolled barrage of fear. It is highly possible that I made mistakes before I left Angela's, that I packed unneeded items, or didn't bring crucial ones. Now, though, I seem to have a revitalised purpose and mindset. I graciously thank whatever happened to me at the bottom of Progress Road. It made me so much stronger.

Water … lots of it, a bag of nappies, and then check the chemist. I grab my mobile phone from inside my coat pocket. *That's strange. It's later than I thought. I must have spent more time at the car showroom than I realised. There's only about an hour of daylight*

152

left, and I need to make Kelly's safe for the night.

Chapter twenty-eight

As Carter falls asleep for the night, safe in my arms, I can hear the anger as they roar outside. They are not too close, away somewhere in the distance.

We are only going to be here for a short amount of time, until tomorrow morning, so I decided to sleep in the back bedroom. It was Amy's when she still lived with her mum.

Another home I love.

I know it was a subconscious choice, powered by familiarity. It also gifts me with an extra degree of security and comfort. I'm even contemplating getting some sleep myself tonight, so that alone proves how much I feel at ease behind these walls. I'm wary about growing complacent, though, and need to stay alert.

The last time I visited Kelly was at the beginning of October. I stopped for a quick cup of tea while I picked up some money for Amy. I walked through the front door on that occasion, however, tonight was a different story. I had to climb over the side gate, retrieve the back door key from under a small pile of bricks, then enter into the kitchen.

"I can't remember what we spoke about, Carter," I whisper, disappointed with my memory. "I know we laughed, though, as we always did."

I lean gently to my right so I can put Carter on the double mattress. I moved it to the floor earlier as I rearranged

154

and fortified areas of the house. It is a skill I seem to have grown proficient at very quickly. I blocked the main doorways, created barriers with furniture and household appliances, and covered up all the windows within forty-five minutes.

Kelly has kept this as a bedroom, a spare one, although she removed Amy's style a few years ago. It now has beige and white walls, and a pine furniture set. There are light-grey borders around both the ceiling and skirting, with a carpet of the same colour to match and compliment. The last time Amy decorated, almost ten years ago, she covered the room in grey brickwork wallpaper. Every piece of furniture was either black and gold, or black and silver.

I let my eyes move around the room, allowing the memories in, and see myself at different ages. I played with dolls and slept in a pink bed, one with a false front that made it look like a princesses castle. I covered my face in make-up, and my body in cool clothes, when my teenage years kicked in. I held my head after Amy's nineteenth birthday, promising never to drink that much brandy ever again.

I enjoy the memories, however, I'm also fighting to stop them from overwhelming me. This room, this house, it's holding me in a warm grasp, welcoming an old friend. It's too much, though, there are too many emotions to deal with. I can almost sense my life around me, yet also have to remember that these people have changed, or are gone forever. The metamorphosis ... the mental evolution that I suffered on Progress Road taught me how to accept these cruel truths, but it doesn't make believing them any less painful.

"I'm going downstairs for a minute, Carter. You'll be safe here. Sleep, baby boy."

I stand up and walk quietly, barefoot, to the top of the stairs. I know where all the creaky floorboards are and step over them carefully.

Shall I run a bath? I really want one, and now would be a

good time. I want to get moving tomorrow morning when the sun rises.

I stand on the small landing for half a minute, unable to make a decision, then head downstairs as I originally intended.

I'm smoking too much, I think as I light a cigarette and sit on the sofa. *I might grab a vape pen tomorrow. I know there are a couple of shops on the way home.*

Apart from Carter's bag, everything else is down here, and I did begin to sort through it all earlier.

You haven't got anything here that you don't actually need. You'll be home tomorrow, does it really matter?

As I stare at the bags and items around the room, I spot Kelly's car keys on the coffee table in front of me. The thought of driving to Southend seems to keep coming back up, as if it is a sign that I should do it. A lot of the roads I've seen have been blocked by the result of damage and violence, but not *all* of them.

I could drive as far as possible towards home. If I do get stuck, though, then what? Walk? Take a different route? Yeah, it's not as complicated as you're making it. Stop overthinking! It will be safe to try it out during the day, right?

"Why didn't you think of this earlier?" I ask myself. I have a disappointed and slightly angry tone, because I *did* think of it earlier. Quite a few times. "Coward!"

Stop it! I didn't know what it was like out there! I couldn't take the risk! I pause for a split second as an unwanted truth tries to break out. ... *Mum ... I want to get home to you, but I fear it so much. I fear the house will be empty when I get home ... I ... I know it will be.*

I don't want to argue with my own mind, not when it is forcing me to accept such harshness, so I stand and begin to inspect the pushchair. I'm hoping for handy buttons, or some very obvious arrow markings, that will teach me how to fold it up.

I should really Google this. It might not even turn into a car seat at all.

I take a few drags on my cigarette, then manage to detach the hood from the pushchair. "Well, that's a good start, right?" I mumble.

Chapter twenty-nine

I exercise, I pamper myself as a reward. The system works, well, mine does.

I love this house because of the sentimental bond it provides. I loved Angela's house, but I hated the car showroom. Until last night, I didn't realise how much I loved the man-cave. Actually, let me be more specific and rephrase that. I love what I found there.

I *did* borrow Kelly's foot spa, I *have* fresh clothes on, and I *definitely* masturbated in the bath as the hot water ran all over my skin. The release was a needed one. *Releases,* plural, if you want total honesty. *So needed.*

I spent roughly half an hour wrestling with Carter's pushchair yesterday evening, and I didn't need to search on Google for instructions either. I worked out all the mechanisms, buttons, clasps, and levers. I won ... eventually.

I stayed in the lounge for a few hours, slowly preparing the bags, and myself, for today's journey. I'm glad that I had tasks to carry out because they kept the dark thoughts locked away, and gave me a positive goal to concentrate on.

I ate an entire pot of chicken pasta that I grabbed from the supermarket, drank a large glass of orange juice, and smoked another couple of cigarettes. I was too tempted to pour out a large glass from the bottle of brandy in the kitchen, however, I resisted. I'd be useless to Carter, and myself, if my head doesn't stay clear.

I know I have found a certain level of clarity, a mental balance, and I don't want to jeopardise that in this now threatening world. The house itself is hindering the endeavour, though, because it possesses an unusual power, one I don't fully understand yet. It is not only a building to me, as I noticed shortly after arriving. I will never regret being here, however, the affection I carry, and the memories, they are a very real danger. In disguise, appearing to me as surreal friends, they're daring me to dream of safety. I am not allowed such luxuries, not yet, and they will only be given on my terms. My newly formed shell of caution must hold off all attacks, especially those cloaked with sentiment and emotion.

As I sat there on the sofa, enjoying some delicious food, it felt strange to me, like it was a normal night at Kelly's. I let my imagination run a couple of times, let myself see her sitting there with me, or standing by the sink in the kitchen. Those are the most dominant memories, and how I will keep her with me.

The thought of taking a bath returned a few times, so I had no choice but to listen. I've definitely noticed a change in myself since Progress Road. I want to bring normality back to my life, I crave any sense of it, and even create instances when I can. Enjoying a cup of tea yesterday, at the car showroom, was a perfect example of this. I would like to believe that it's because acceptance has finally become my new companion, as opposed to terror.

It should have been simple to run a bath, however, it turned into a long list of tasks and over half an hour of repetitive work. I couldn't just turn the taps on, and Charlie's voice didn't even appear inside my head with another warning about the water supply.

I need to learn a lot for the future, so much. Collecting rain, sterilisation techniques, converting sea water like those survival experts on the television. There's no other way.

I daydreamed about emptying every shop and

supermarket of all their bottled water. It's a plausible idea now, and one I will build on and refine in the weeks and months to come. The sell-by date on the water bottle labels gives me between eight and nine months, so I have time to plan.

There are loads of shops near home, and some supermarkets as well. I could easily fill a trolley, or a car if I can get it there, quite a few times in one day.

I raided Kelly's kitchen cupboards for all the saucepans she owns, filled them with bottled water, then started to boil them up on the oven hobs. I think I used about ten of them in the end. I grabbed as many as I could while in the supermarket and crammed them in the bags. I shoved a few more under the pushchair as well, until I had no space left whatsoever. I even managed to carry two under my arm and steer one-handed.

Once boiled, I carefully carried the water upstairs to the bath and poured it in. It sounds ridiculous, but I was actually terrified. I thought the water was making too much noise, that it would attract the anger straight to Kelly's.

Courtesy of Kelly's bathroom supplies, I ended up with about two inches of fragrant and bubble-covered water. The downside to it all was a slight burn on my already damaged wrist. A random splash of freshly boiled water caught me. It was worth it, though, so worth it.

I grabbed some body wash from my bag, shampoo, one of Kelly's unused razors, and a new toothbrush I took from the chemist up the road. I used one of the saucepans to gently pour the water over my head and body, always slowly, so there wasn't any sound. It was amazing. The hot water, aromatic scents, and the feel of the smooth lather on my skin. I could record an advertisement video right now for all the companies involved.

'Every other person in the world disappeared? Are you hunted by psychotic, raging beasts? Have you been walking around the dirty streets lately, surrounded by death and decay? Don't worry! Use our coconut shampoo and passion flower body wash, and you'll be revitalised in no time!'

I fed Carter at about seven o'clock this morning, nearly twenty-five minutes ago. We watched out of the window as the sky turned a lighter grey, coloured with a very subtle pink and orange. It was as if a watercolour artist was painting the scene before our very eyes.

Sunrise. We're free again, Carter. It's our world now, and we can finally make it home.

"I've got a wonderful surprise for you today, Carter," I say as I stare at his glistening and beautiful eyes.

His adorable reply is to yawn, smile, then gently stroke across my arm with his fingers.

"We're going to borrow Kelly's car and go for a drive! Yes we are! I'm going to take you to your new house. Your new …" I choke back some tears. "… your new home."

I ran the mathematics through my head while waiting for the sun to rise. Here at Kelly's, we are about three miles away from my house. If I'm only travelling at ten miles per hour all the way there, crawling along in the low gears, I'll reach home in about twenty minutes. I'm expecting a couple of detours, minimum, but it is so close. I will … *we* will be home today.

"Aavooah!" screams Carter with a kick of his legs.

I love how he mimics my enthusiasm, or reacts exactly as I need him to do, even though he doesn't properly understand. It is such a boost of confidence to see him act in such a way. It proves to me that I'm not actually an exhausted, useless, and shitty protector, despite my fears.

"I know, it's so exciting!"

He shakes one of his toys at me, a soft lion made of orange and yellow fabrics.

That reminds me …

"Oh, you are so right, little man, I did promise you some toys, didn't I? I won't forget. As soon as the car is ready for you, we are leaving."

••

I sit down in the driver's seat of Kelly's car, a dark-grey Mercedes, and tell myself that I'm not going to be sick. It hasn't been long since I ate breakfast, but it's made my stomach start to ache. I chose a yoghurt and a banana this morning, and I have eaten when possible in the past week, but it hasn't been the healthiest diet. I think my body is trying to warn me that it doesn't agree with the new routine.

I must have been so determined to get inside yesterday because I didn't pay any attention to the state of the nearby houses. I can't even recall what it was like walking here from the shops. There are a few smashed windows, open doors, and damaged cars. It looks as if this area escaped the full force of the anger, and that grants me some slight relief. I want all that I hold close to be safe, untouched, and remain pure.

Now, it hasn't been that long since you've been in a car. You can do this. You can drive, and you can drive all the way home. Take it slow, be safe.

Carter is strapped into his baby travel seat, warm and safe, however, he has been a little bit upset over the last half an hour. There were a couple of short episodes of frustrated moans, and he hasn't smiled as much as usual either. I ran through Tammie's 'why-is-the-baby-crying' list, and worked on all the possible reasons.

Remember what you thought about at the man-cave? He might just be sensing your fears. You are scared, anxious, excited about going home, but terrified of it at the same time.

It's a valid theory. It's *more* than a valid theory. It's probably ninety-nine point nine percent truth.

I get back out of the car, open the rear door, then lean through to face him in the middle of the back seats.

"We're going to be fine, little man, okay? Whatever happens today, we will be fine."

I smile, poke my tongue out, then tickle Carter above his knee. "We have each other, right? Shayla and Carter, together for an adventure!"

I reach inside his bag, next to him on the left seat, and grab the blue elephant toy.

"Look, Carter! Your elephant friend is here! I think he wants to have another chat with you. Are you going to talk to your friend? Are you?" I ask, my voice playful and full of excitement.

"Aaayaa," he whispers with a smile.

My stomach eases as I get back in the driver's seat. I've noticed that when I am concentrating on Carter, specifically his happiness or well-being, I ignore my own fears.

I start the car and sit for another few minutes, keeping my mind as calm as possible. The sun beams down on the car and through the windows, warms my body, and fuels my positivity. It is mild outside this morning and the patches of blue sky are a welcome addition, a change to the usual grey overhead.

I'll come back, Kelly. I'll make a promise now, just as you and Mum did all those years ago. Whenever I can, I will visit this house.

I push down on the brake pedal, move the gear lever to 'D', and slowly lift my foot. The car creeps forward as I steer slightly to the right and, with anticipation and hope in my heart, start the final part of our journey.

"Off we go, Carter. I'm right here if you need me, but I do have to concentrate on driving, though."

A gentle murmur is my simple response. I expect he's too busy with the blue elephant again to pay attention to what I'm saying.

Within twenty seconds I have reached the end of Kelly's road. My heart is beating ridiculously fast, I'm grinding my teeth again, and my hands are gripped too tightly on the steering wheel.

The garden wall on the other side of the street is stained with blood. "Come on, you're okay. You're heading home," I whisper to myself. "Whatever happened there, it's over now."

I hope.

I turn right and increase my speed as I head up the hill section of Elmsleigh Drive. My eyes flick from left to right. I can't ignore the damage to the houses, fences, and cars, but I do try.

"Isn't this … this great? Are you and your elephant friend having lots of fun in the car?" I ask as I reach a set of traffic lights, a junction in the road. My voice is shaking ever so slightly.

Carter doesn't answer me. I stop the car and think about which road to take next.

Straight ahead … or left?

I move the gear lever to 'P', stick the handbrake on, then lean through to the back. It's slightly awkward for me because Carter's rear-facing seat is in my way.

"Boo!"

Carter smiles widely and grabs his elephant even tighter. "Ooooh!"

"Just checking in on you, baby boy."

I move back to my seat, put the car back in 'drive', and continue to think both options through. I can only see a few obstructions in view on either of the roads.

The hospital is on the left, further up the road. I don't think I want to go near that, though. I don't know why, but it doesn't feel … safe.

I drive forward, steer carefully around a pile of snapped fence panels, and head on. I can see the London Road in front of me, up another hill.

Left at the lights … left at the lights and straight home!

"Don't worry, Carter, I haven't forgotten about the toys. We'll stop in a couple of minutes and throw some stuff in the car."

I'll get Mum some flowers. No, wait, that's a stupid idea! Erm … chocolate! Yeah, chocolate! Tea bags as well … and a new kettle …

I turn left to join the London Road, however, I have to stop after only a few seconds. There is a smashed up lorry in front of me, its interior almost completely destroyed by a past fire. The once white paintwork is blistered and a dull grey, streaked with black smoke lines. The remains of the front seats, dashboard, and steering wheel look skeletal.

Typical! I should have gone the other way! Shall I quickly turn around and drive back? No, wait … There's enough room to get the car around it, if I'm careful.

Suddenly, an image punches its way through my mind. A fire. It is so vivid, so clear, I am caught by the overpowering intensity and cannot get it out of my head.

Why am I thinking about this? What is it? I don't … don't …

More follow in a random sequence. I recognise one of the thoughts, although it is distorted, somehow altered. It's the car showroom I passed through yesterday afternoon, however, one of the vehicles is now on fire. The front seat is covered in flames. They're crackling and spreading rapidly inside the chassis, climbing across the inside of the roof, and dancing up the windows.

I saw that car … that was the black estate that we looked at. I don't understand this! Why am I seeing this now? Why has it changed so much?

"There wasn't any fire. There wasn't any fire," I say. I don't know why this is scaring me, but it is.

The unwanted images change. I'm on the other side of the Arterial Road, staring back at the showroom. I'm staring back at the tall windows, and I can just make out a plume of dark-grey smoke drifting around inside the building.

"That didn't happen! It didn't … it didn't."

Chapter thirty

I reach the corner of Chalkwell Park a few minutes later and stop the car. The road is blocked again by a few fallen traffic light posts, some metal fencing that used to border the field, and the twisted frames of two telephone boxes. I know I can't get by it in the car this time, though, the remains cover from one side of the street to the other. I'm reminded of the barrier, the wall of hope, that I saw on Eastwood Road, albeit on a much smaller scale.

Park the car.

I put the gear lever in the 'park' position.

Handbrake.

I lift the handbrake.

Take a moment to plan the new route.

My mind goes blank.

There are mounds of glass on the road as well, as was the case with Rayleigh High Street. The shops nearby have no front windows any longer, so it's easy to work out where it all came from. I am surrounded once again by clusters of diamonds, and they are all gracing the moment with their beauty.

'After traumatic events, the memory can become distorted, Shayla. You saw a burnt out van a moment ago, then your mind mixed it with what you experienced yesterday. Trust me, I'm a scientist … and …,' begins Charlie. Her words are delivered in a soft and understanding voice.

"What?" I ask.

'… and I'm your friend. I'm always your friend.'

I stay silent as I get out of the car. I need Carter close to me. I need him to save me from my own doubt, and hold my hand as I teeter on the edge. His soft touch, always full of warmth, will force me to stay in the real world.

The pool of blood … it hasn't called to me for a long time. Perhaps this is it? The moment I fall, forever?

The damage around this area is far reaching, extensive, and unimaginably violent. A section of the roof from a nearby house is missing, and the school building to my right has an entire chunk of its corner wall smashed away. I can see, with a crushed heart, PE equipment, paintings on the inside walls, and low chairs.

There are a few dead foxes over there, by the entrance to the park. I haven't seen many animals, well, I can't remember seeing any, and when did I last hear any birdsong?

'My friend, *you*, wouldn't have done something so … so malicious. You must know that?'

I get in the back of the car and Carter smiles when he sees me. His little legs kick about as he wriggles in the travel seat.

I did want to hurt them. I really felt it … so strong … They … they made me fight back.

"Thank you, baby boy," I say as a few tears fall down my face. I force a smile of my own so that I don't upset him.

"Come on. Shall we have a cuddle?"

I will not fall off the edge … I will not. Fight it with me, Carter … fight it with me …

I undo the clasps and take Carter out of the seat, straight into a tight embrace. His face feels warm and soft against mine, and his scent is intoxicating to me right now.

"I might have done it. I was … was angry enough. I don't remember. I lost time again. Anything could have happened!"

167

Carter grabs at my face, then starts to gently nibble and chew at my cheek. He doesn't have a clue what I'm talking about and is enjoying the opportunity for affection.

'Yes, you might have, Shayla, but you *didn't*,' insists Charlie. 'You are going to have to believe it yourself, or you'll never be able to let this go. I mean, why do you think I'm here now? Why am I a voice inside your head? I'm your truth, that's why.'

I reciprocate the loving gesture and kiss Carter on the cheek, then stare at his eyes. They are so beautiful in the sunshine, almost hypnotic, made of pure gold.

"Look at all this damage and mess, Carter. We can't drive straight through here, it's impossible." I pause, severely disappointed because I can almost see the building I want to reach. "I'll go around the outside of the park, then back up to the shop that way. Good idea?"

He is too preoccupied with chewing my face to answer the question, or give me any of his usual opinions.

'Go home, Shayla. Go home. You have to believe me, *and* you have to believe in yourself.'

I put Carter back in his travel seat, then give him and his elephant animated and overly affectionate kisses, complete with loud 'Mwah!' sounds.

As I hoped it would, a chuckle of laughter bursts out. If anything can save me from worrying about being an arsonist, possibly a killer as well, it is that magnificent reaction.

I … I really wanted to hurt them … to fight back … hurt … hurt them …

I expect tears are falling, yet I can't feel them on my numb and cold skin.

••

I'm surprised, and relieved, to see that the small supermarket hasn't been damaged by the anger.

I need to work out their … their behaviour pattern. I have to!

What drives them to destroy and attack? I know they're attracted to any sound or noise, infuriated by it, but why rip cars apart? Smashed up walls and traffic lights don't make a sound! Unless it is … completely random? Rage, pure and mindless. There is no pattern to discover.

"It's like … erm … some sort of a … primal … reverse evolution," I say, picking words out of my confused mind. "What do you think?"

Carter giggles and smiles at me from the baby seat of the supermarket trolley. I had to prop him in place with the help of one of the knitted jumpers from my bag. He's too young to have mastered the 'sitting' skill yet, so now he is safe, comfortable, and can't lean too far in any direction.

"Of course, you would think this is hilarious," I say through my own laugh. "Werewolves? Aaawwooo!"

Smiles and laughter.

"Vampires?" I snap my teeth together a couple of times.

Shrieks of delight.

"Drunk scientist accidentally unleashes a mutation virus that spreads across the globe in a matter of days, only sparing us two?"

Wild kicks of the legs, wide eyes, and shakes of his head.

"You like that one the best? Okay, baby boy, then that is what happened," I say in a joking tone. It is feigned because I want to know the actual reason. I want to be shocked, disgusted, and full of disbelief. At least I'll know the absolute truth.

Seeing as Carter can't hold his body upright properly, he loses balance, wobbles forward, then plants his face into my soft jumper.

"Oh no! What did you do?" I say, laughing gently. I move him back, rearrange my jumper, then give him a quick kiss.

More of our new memories together, joyous and positive ones. Don't let them go. Use them to push the bad thoughts away, until you

169

can believe Charlie, and yourself. You know you already do. If you search inside your mind, then you know she's right.

"She is my truth," I whisper.

She has been since the first time you heard her voice, since she began to help you and push your mind. Always there, always calm, helping you to find the ...

"... the truth. My truth. My thoughts, her voice."

I've known this since the man-cave. I've known that Charlie is only a projection of my mind, created to think the unthinkable questions, and forge ahead so I had no choice but to follow. She ignored me there ... *I ignored myself.* I knew why, but I didn't want to admit it. I didn't want to risk her voice disappearing forever if I lowered the veil.

I walk through the automatic doors and stop after only a few steps, just to get my bearings. I have shopped here in the past, but I have no idea where anything is.

Why does it smell so strange? It reminds me of ... of ... oh, it's Joan's greenhouse at the bottom of her garden. Yeah, at the height of the summer.

I dab the menthol rub under my nose again, and on the leg of Carter's body suit as well.

It must be coming from down there, on the fruit and vegetable aisle. Some of it will have started to rot by now.

"Right, Carter, are you ready?" I ask. "We're going to do some shopping. You can help me, yeah? Don't let me get distracted, or forget anything important."

Carter looks left and right, up and around. His eyes are overloaded by all the colours and lights inside, *plus* the toys close to him.

"Ooh, look at all these!" I squeal, immediately distracted, ignoring my own instructions. "There are Christmas teddy bears here! We have a reindeer, a polar bear, a ... erm ... what is that? Is it a squirrel?"

I grab the stuffed animal off of the shelf and inspect it first. The tag states that it is suitable from birth, so I'm satisfied it's a safe toy for Carter to play with. It is made of

170

light-grey and purple fabric, with lilac eyes. I'm stuck between whether it is a fox that has decided to stand up, or a squirrel as I first assumed.

Go with squirrel.

"What shall we call it?" I say as I pull the tag off and hand it over. "I think it's definitely a girl squirrel. We are going to need a beautiful name for her, Carter."

"Hmma."

"Well, let's think about it while we do some shopping, okay?" I suggest as I look at all the other toys and decorations. I grab a pair of novelty reindeer antlers that flash with red and green lights, and a set of four cinnamon and pine candles.

Mum loved this scent, I think. I don't correct myself after using the past tense.

Carter approves of the teddy, regardless of what animal it is supposed to be. He grabbed it and immediately started chewing on one of the ears. I take that to mean he loves our new squirrel friend, even though her appearance is a little bit garish.

The tobacco checkout is on the far wall to my right, so I head there and push the trolley to one side.

"We'll start here, then go along all the aisles, yeah? Grab everything, then go. Grab, go! Grab, go!"

I speak in a silly voice and reach for Carter with wriggling fingers. "Grab, grab, grab!"

He kicks about with excitement, smiles, then squeezes the as of yet unnamed squirrel very close to his body.

I climb on the counter and drop down the other side. The shutter in front of all the cigarettes isn't locked, so I push it out of the way and start to grab boxes.

Carter's eyes follow my rushed and random movements, and he seems fascinated by the gentle 'thump' as they land in the trolley.

I open a box and light a cigarette as I continue to loot. I probably should care more about the fact that I'm stealing, but I don't, not at all.

Rolling tobacco, papers, a few lighters, and even more boxes of cigarettes get thrown in. I don't worry about smoking too much this time, as I did at Kelly's.

Vaping pens. Get a few of them ... and some liquid as well. Hurry up, though! There's more to do.

I climb back on the counter and sit for a second. I want to try and stay relaxed while I am in here, only get what I need, but I know that I'm back to making lots of frantic movements again.

Aisle by aisle. Finish your cigarette, then do it.

I listen to my advice and take a moment. I don't actually want to because I fear the thoughts I had earlier will return.

I do believe in myself, and Charlie. I do believe. I ... I couldn't do that, not even to the anger. They didn't ask for this. They were like me until last week ... normal human beings. I have to believe they still are, somewhere inside.

'That's good to hear,' she replies. 'Besides, it doesn't even add up, so it must be a distortion of your memory. You had to search for the cigarette lighter on the way across the road. It was inside one of the bags, not your hand or coat pocket. Your body and clothes would have reeked of smoke until you changed and took a bath at Kelly's. *They didn't,* did they?'

"No ... and thank you, Charlie. Thank you for, you know ..."

'For what?'

"Staying with me. Being my friend when I needed you the most."

'I told you earlier, didn't I? I am your friend. That will never change, Shayla.'

"Voonah," says Carter as he stares at me. He grows a beaming smile and holds up the squirrel toy.

"Vuna?" I say. "That sounds like Luna. I love it! Welcome to the family, Vuna."

172

I throw my finished cigarette on the floor, then stub it out with my boot as I jump down off of the counter.

"Right, we need food. Let's go." I clap my hands together. "Carter, Vuna, are you with me?"

Vuna is understandably quiet, while Carter squeals at me through rapid breaths. He has behaved in a similar way in the past. It seems like he is building up to let out a monumental scream, one that never quite makes it out of his mouth.

The first shelf I look at is stocked full of alcohol, and all the soft drinks are opposite. I grab a couple of bottles of brandy, some Pepsi, then move swiftly on.

Sugar ... yeah ... eggs ... erm?

I stare at the boxes of eggs and think about sell-by dates again, as I did with the water. Then, with gritted teeth because I have annoyed myself, I imagine opening one of the bottles of brandy to calm myself down.

A lot of this stuff will already be out of date, or very close to it. Fuck! This isn't going to be as easy as I first thought. Fuck it!

I have no idea why, but I stick my middle finger up at a box of eggs on the shelf.

"Whatever!"

I grind my teeth, then turn around to the freezers behind me. They restore my calmness once my eyes see date stamps for months ahead in the future. I start to ignore what the actual food is and only look at the numbers.

Okay ... good. This will work ... it will, I think as I light another cigarette. I make sure to push Carter a couple of feet along the aisle, away from me and the smoke.

"Pizza, pasta meals, lasagna, burgers, fish ... fish fingers ... nuggets. I'll get the lot, Carter! All of it!"

I grab boxes, as many as I can balance in my arms, and take them to the trolley. My mind wants to plan in months, my hands for a week. They want this done, and they want it done quickly.

I reach the back wall, a long line of chilled cabinets

spanning the entire width of the shop. They are covered in meats, plus some dairy as well. I don't even bother to look, already knowing it isn't worth my time, and head up the second aisle.

"No, not there. Round the corner ... woooohooo!" I turn the trolley in a full circle, gently, and smile widely at Carter. I might be frustrated because so much of the food in here is useless, but he doesn't have to share my annoyance.

"Tea bags!" I shout as my eyes scan the top shelf. I take far too many boxes and ignore the rest of the dairy opposite.

At the other end of the aisle, I stop and refocus. "Ahh, now this is important, Carter. This is all the stuff you will need."

"Hnnava."

"Yeah, nappies, formula milk ... ooh, new dummies as well!"

Household items fill the next aisle, so I grab a couple of the ever important kettles that I wanted. They're brand new and, more importantly, unused. I smile as I see the cutlery a couple feet away, especially the selection of knives. I have to pick up a cleaver, despite the fact I am so attached to the one from Amy's kitchen.

The final aisle is glorious and terrible at exactly the same time, as if an invisible line has been drawn directly down its centre.

I was right about the smell earlier, when I first walked in. It is coming from here.

One side is fruit, vegetables, bread, and other baked goods, all of which are worthless to me in the long run. The other is boxed or packaged cereal, rices, pastas, and tinned goods.

"Last few bits, little man, then ... home," I say, my voice cracking on the word 'home'.

Carter spins his head around to see where the noise made by the various tins is coming from. They clash with the metal frame of the trolley and send echoing notes through the supermarket.

I take a lot. I can't remember why the thought is in my head, but post-apocalyptic survival usually hinges on how many tins of beans you have available to eat.

"That's it! Done!" I say with an accomplished tone.

On the way out of the supermarket, I throw an extra couple of squirrels in the trolley. I'll feel much more relaxed knowing that Carter will always have Vuna near him.

Chapter thirty-one

I throw in the last boxes of cigarettes, slam the boot of the car shut, then rush to Carter. He's already in his travel seat in the back, smiling and chatting.

"Five minutes, little man. Only five minutes to go."

My voice lowers to almost a whisper as I speak the words. I kiss his cheek, tickle his knee, and smile back at him with as much honesty as is possible.

I can do this. I can. I … can walk through the front door, no matter what.

I move the gear lever to 'drive', pull out of the car park, then head right. There is a dark cloud overhead and I push all my positive thoughts to the forefront of my mind. I do not want to see it, *and believe in it*, as a bad omen.

Okay, get to Crowstone Road.

"You alright back there, little man?" I ask as I slow down and steer to the left. There's a bench in the road that I need to avoid. I realise it has been ripped out of the ground and thrown from outside the nearby library.

I hear a gentle hum from Carter in reply. I hope Vuna is still close by, providing the comfort and distraction he needs. In a rather selfish sense, if he isn't crying, I won't stop until I reach my house.

I turn right, heading towards Genesta Road. My foot is desperate to push down hard on the accelerator pedal, yet I somehow resist and fight my wavering patience.

Minutes away ... minutes ... stay safe ... think of Carter.

I look at the speedometer and readjust from forty to thirty miles per hour. The desire to finally reach home is extremely powerful, almost ordering me to behave in a reckless and nonchalant manner.

Left here, along to Valkyrie.

I manage to travel down the road for about ten more seconds before I have to stop the car.

No way ...

There is a large dog, a black Great Dane, in the middle of the road. It is very much alive, and rummaging one of its paws through a ripped open bin bag. The cloud I saw earlier has moved away, so the sun bounces off of its glossy coat.

I haven't seen a dog in ... well, in ages! The anger hasn't killed everything. Not yet, I think, elated by this unusual sight.

The dog turns its attention to me and barks a couple of times. They are deep because of the breed, and send booming echoes across the empty street.

Survivors. We're all survivors.

I actually let the thought of taking the dog home enter my head, unsure if I can leave it abandoned. It lingers for a few seconds as I contemplate the idea, then I slowly drive around it with feelings of sorrow and guilt. I have felt selfish many times in the past week, however, those experiences have not made it any less unbearable.

I turn right onto Valkyrie Road, then left almost immediately after. *Crowstone Road. Through the lights and all the way along until the school.*

I'm familiar with the area, these are the streets I see almost daily, so my mind is rushing ahead of my physical body. My peripheral vision blurs and I can only focus on what is directly ahead of me.

So close. So close. Just get there!

I lose unnecessary thoughts from my mind, and I don't care about anything else. I don't care about the damage around me. I don't care for what the anger have done to my neighbourhood.

Turn right, Westcliff Avenue.

A tear rolls down my cheek as the most intense anticipation I've ever sensed turns darker. Atrocious images are created, centred on Mum, *and* what will happen when I walk through my front door.

No! No! Please! I want this out of my head ... get it out of my fucking head!

I push on the brakes with force and the car stops immediately. I was only travelling at ten miles per hour, maybe less.

I'm going to be sick ...

I manage to get the door open and lean out as my stomach stabs and cramps with gripping pulses. I retch and vomit on the road as my hands grab at the steering wheel and edge of the seat.

Please ... please ... I can't see this ...

"Galla. Hmmma."

Carter ...

I take a deep breath in, hold it for a couple of seconds, then let it out very slowly. "You're okay. You are," I say, reassuring myself as I sit back up in the seat.

"Hmma!"

I turn around to see that Vuna has fallen out of reach. Carter is looking at her, just inches in front of him, with an upset look on his face.

"Don't worry, baby boy." I wipe the tears of my face and catch another breath. "I'll save her for you."

I lean through from the front, give Vuna back to Carter, then simply stare at him. I trace the curves on and around his face, watch the sunlight on his skin, and smile as his golden eyes fixate on the toy squirrel.

'Ready?' asks Charlie.

"Yeah ... I'm ready," I whisper as the car moves gently forward again.

I turn left a couple of seconds later and join Cambridge road.

Cambridge Road.

I live on Cambridge Road.

My road.

Home.

I veer right at a small roundabout and my eyes widen when I see the deep-green leaves of a large Camellia shrub. I see it every day across the road from my house.

My blinkered eyesight suddenly normalises, then overcompensates. Everything in view becomes well-defined, has crisp edges, and the world is alive and pulsating with vibrant colours. Small shards of glass on the road catch the sunlight, tall trees lining the paths appear so pastel and artistic, and the sky itself is an unending blue canvas.

"The one with the white fence."

My words dance on a breath. I see the house to my left.

"C ... Carter ..."

"Vooah."

"We're ... we're home."

I stop the car and turn off the engine, however, instead of rushing out, I keep my eyes slightly down at the steering wheel. I want to look at the lounge window so much. I want to look and see her there, crying with happiness. My neck physically hurts because I am holding my body so still and rigid.

Get out of the car.

I get out of the car.

Grab Carter.

I open the car door and take Carter out of his travel seat.

Look up. Look up.

I raise my head as many tears begin to flow. She isn't there. Mum isn't there.

Inside ... I can, remember? I can walk through the front door,

179

no matter what.

I begin to walk up the townhouse steps, surprised by the lack of damage. I can't move fast, however, I'm unsure if I actually want to. I have a couple of vague memories in my head, more feelings than actual thoughts. I couldn't move when I first left Amy's because my legs lost their strength, and fear paralysed me outside Angela's. This is exactly the same. Crushing hesitation causes my feet and leg muscles to feel numb and useless. Every step I take leads to a few seconds of inactivity because my boots are weighed down, stuck on the stone beneath me.

Carter is unaware of my inner struggle. He looks around, sucks on his dummy, and takes in the new and exciting surroundings. The bushes, trees, vehicles, and the fronts of all the houses provide a multitude of colours.

I stare at my own front door. I have begged to be here for a week, and have suffered in unimaginable ways to return.

Another few seconds … that's all I need.

My eyes examine the deep-red paintwork, brass letterbox, knocker, and handle. I cleaned them all only a few weeks ago because Mum was ill with a cold.

That's enough. You have to do this.

I kiss Carter, then lean forward and push on the front door.

It's locked. Is … is that a good thing? I … erm … need my keys. Yeah, keys. Where are my keys? Where are my fucking keys!

I ram my hand into the pockets of my coat, however, I don't find what I'm looking for.

Seriously? SHIT!

I rush back down the steps, open the driver's seat of the car, then recline it as far as I can.

"Okay, little man, you rest there while Shayla goes through her handbag. Silly Shayla doesn't know where her door keys are."

Think! Thinkthinkthinkthinkthink!

Carter looks adorable as he kicks and waves, so I afford myself a needed moment of laughter, happiness, and clarity.

I hear the glorious 'clink' sound of keys touching each other, grab whatever is near my hand, then yank it out of the bag.

In the split second before I see the small bunch of keys in my palm, I drop the unneeded junk on the passenger seat. There's a pot of lip gloss, half a pack of mints, and Susan's lighter.

'I told you, didn't I?' gloats Charlie.

I return to the front door, push the key in the lock, then slowly open it.

Mum?

"Mum," I whisper.

I move forward with a couple of heavy steps, although I feel as if I am gliding above the burgundy carpet. I'm a long dead spirit, visiting its former home. The sensation pulsing through my body is indescribable. Something is crawling all over my skin, scraping at my bones, and freezing the blood in my veins.

Mum?

"Mum?!" I yell.

The silence forces me to my knees, and I comply without any resistance. I know the tears are there, swimming beneath my eyes, yet they won't fall. I am trapped on the edge of sadness, destined to live there forever. When I can accept the loss, the truth I have fought for so many days, *and only then*, I will grieve and begin to heal.

"I'm sorry, Mum. I'm so sorry."

The journey is finally over, yet my heart is broken, as is my mind.

As I lean against the wall, my embrace tightens. I bring Carter closer to me, stare at his golden eyes, and give myself permission to see more of our future together.

I need it. Do you understand, baby boy? I need it so much, or I can't go on.

"There's no other way," I say as my eyes lock with Carter's. "I'll take it."

Chapter thirty-two

The possibility of an epilogue

I open my eyes and look around my bedroom. My hands immediately check my arms for intravenous tubes, and my mouth for a breathing pipe.

No. You're not in a coma. You are alive. It happened. It is still happening.

I roll over on the mattress and stare at Carter's face. He is angelic when asleep, as if sculpted out of the finest marble.

Say the words.

I sit up and stare at the walls, ceiling, door, and window. They are all covered in several layers of thick fabric.

Say the words.

I grab my mobile phone. There is a notification on the screen, letting me know that sunrise occurred four minutes ago.

Say the words. Say them!

"She has gone. Mum. My mum. She has gone."

I stare at the wall to my right. There are words on it that I painted seven months ago, a few days after I returned here. I speak them as a gentle thought in my mind.

Now survive another day. Survive for him.

THE END